BOOK FOUR

HAMMERED

USA TODAY BESTSELLING AUTHOR

HEATHER SLADE

HAMMERED
© 2022 Heather Slade

This book is a work of fiction. The names, characters, places and incidents are products of the writer's imagination or have been used fictitiously and are not to be construed as real. Any resemblance to persons, living or dead, actual events, locale or organizations is entirely coincidental.

979-8-88649-142-5

hammered
/ˈhamer'd/
verb
utterly defeat; trounce;
bring someone to their knees

MORE FROM AUTHOR HEATHER SLADE

BUTLER RANCH
Kade's Worth
Brodie's Promise
Maddox's Truce
Naughton's Secret
Mercer's Vow
Kade's Return
Butler Ranch Christmas

WICKED WINEMAKERS
FIRST LABEL
Brix's Bid
Ridge's Release
Press' Passion
Zin's Sins
Tryst's Temptation

WICKED WINEMAKERS
SECOND LABEL
Beau's Beloved
Coming Soon:
Cru's Crush
Bones' Bliss
Snapper's Seduction
Kick's Kiss

ROARING FORK RANCH
Coming Soon:
Roaring Fork Wrangler
Roaring Fork Roughstock
Roaring Fork Rockstar
Roaring Fork Rooker
Roaring Fork Bridger

THE ROYAL AGENTS
OF MI6
Make Me Shiver
Drive Me Wilder
Feel My Pinch
Chase My Shadow
Find My Angel

K19 SECURITY
SOLUTIONS TEAM ONE
Razor's Edge
Gunner's Redemption
Mistletoe's Magic
Mantis' Desire
Dutch's Salvation

K19 SECURITY
SOLUTIONS TEAM TWO
Striker's Choice
Monk's Fire
Halo's Oath
Tackle's Honor
Onyx's Awakening

K19 SHADOW OPERATIONS
TEAM ONE
Code Name: Ranger
Code Name: Diesel
Code Name: Wasp
Code Name: Cowboy
Code Name: Mayhem

K19 ALLIED INTELLIGENCE
TEAM ONE
Code Name: Ares
Code Name: Cayman
Code Name: Poseidon
Code Name: Zeppelin
Code Name: Magnet

K19 ALLIED INTELLIGENCE
TEAM TWO
Coming Soon:
Code Name: Puck
Code Name: Michelangelo
Code Name: Typhon
Code Name: Hornet
Code Name: Reaper

PROTECTORS
UNDERCOVER
Undercover Agent
Undercover Emissary
Coming Soon:
Undercover Savior
Undercover Infidel
Undercover Assassin

THE INVINCIBLES
TEAM ONE
Decked
Edged
Grinded
Riled
Smoked

THE INVINCIBLES
TEAM TWO
Bucked
Irished
Sainted
Hammered
Ripped

THE UNSTOPPABLES
TEAM ONE
Furied
Merried

COWBOYS OF
CRESTED BUTTE
A Cowboy Falls
A Cowboy's Dance
A Cowboy's Kiss
A Cowboy Stays
A Cowboy Wins

Table of Contents

1

Hammer

My phone vibrated with a text message. *Urgent I speak with you ASAP,* it read.

A few minutes ago, when I saw Kellen "Money" McTiernan's name show up on my cell shortly after my flight landed at Austin-Bergstrom, I let it go to voicemail. What could he possibly need to talk to me about now? It hadn't been that long since we went our separate ways after traveling to DC from London. We'd both been there for our mutual friends Saint and Harper's New Year's Eve wedding celebration. Not to mention, it was eight in the morning and I hadn't gotten any sleep on either plane ride.

"Fuck," I muttered under my breath, wishing I could wait until I'd gotten some rest to respond but knowing ignoring him was out of the question.

As the Invincibles' attorney of record, I had no choice but to answer when one of them called—urgent or not. While McTiernan didn't work for them, he was the director of the CIA as well as our primary contact there, which meant he counted.

"What can I do for you?" I asked when Money picked up.

"My sister needs help."

She better be in lockup for him to send me a message saying it was urgent he speak with me after I'd just traveled all night. "What's going on?"

"She's buying a bar not far from where you are—one I told her not to, in fact—and evidently, the owner tried to renegotiate the sale last night."

"And?"

"She shot him."

"Which bar?"

"The Long Branch."

Now I understood why Money told her not to buy it. As far as law-abiding citizens went, more of their customers weren't than were.

The place was less than fifteen minutes away on the outskirts of Austin, Texas, my hometown. It was owned by Bobby MacIver, only brother of John, the sheriff of Hays County. This oughta be fun. *Real fun.*

"Lemme call you when I get to my office. Should be about thirty minutes."

"Copy that. Thanks, Hammer."

"Yep." I ended the call, pulled the cigar case out of my breast pocket, and took out my stogie. I never smoked the thing. I used it more as a prop than anything. It was different back when I was with the Marine Raider Regiment. After a mission with them or Force Recon, I needed four fingers of bourbon and a couple of Cubans to settle me down.

I studied the cigar that had seen better days. Once I got home later, I'd pull a new one out of the humidor.

"Hey, Mac," I said when the sheriff answered my call.

"Been waiting to hear from you."

"Yeah?"

"You know I have. Guess McTiernan filled you in."

"You wanna tell me why the director of the CIA called me after he was on the same red-eye flight I was, saying his sister needed help?"

"Don't play chicken with me, Hammer. You know damn well why."

"All he said was that his sister shot your brother."

"That isn't all. We got her locked up on all kinds of shit. A couple unpaid speeding tickets, possession of a firearm in an establishment that derives more than fifty-one percent of its revenue from alcohol…"

I rolled my eyes. He could've just said "a bar." I was certainly aware of the law.

"The kicker, though, is attempted murder."

"Wait a minute. Attempted murder? Was it really that bad?"

"Well, now, Hammer, that comes down to a case of he said/she said, and she did shoot him."

"Where?"

"In the leg."

"Money said Bobby tried to renegotiate the sale."

"Can't imagine any judge or jury would consider that enough of a reason to shoot someone. Anyway, we've got her in the county jail. Probably won't see the judge until tomorrow. Maybe the next day."

I could find out on my own, but it was easier to ask if Mac knew. "Have you heard what the DA is thinking about asking for the bond amount?"

"At least a million bucks."

"What? Why?"

"Forgot to mention she had one or two outstanding bench warrants. Anyway, you wanna know what I wanna know?"

"I can hardly wait."

"How in blazes did two parents raise such different kids? One's the director of a national intelligence agency, and the other's practically a career criminal."

"I'm anxious to get that answer myself."

"Talk later, Counselor."

"Thanks, Mac."

I pulled up to the gates of my thousand-acre piece of land in Dripping Springs and waited for them to open. It wasn't like I kept a lot of valuables in the nine-hundred-square-foot house the property came with. No, it was more my affiliation with the Invincibles that meant I had to keep security damn tight.

If those assholes would let me stay put for a few days, maybe I could actually move into the house I was having built to replace the shack I lived in now. It wasn't finished yet, but was probably far enough along for me to make it work—if I ever had the time.

As it was, the original house suited me okay. I had a grill. I had a kitchen too, but I didn't use it much for cooking. Usually, I wasn't here for meals anyway.

Otherwise, the place had a shower, a living room, and a bedroom. What else did a single guy who was never home need?

I tossed my bag on my bed, tired enough that all I wanted to do was sleep until tomorrow morning, but I knew I couldn't. Nope, after I talked to ol' Money, I was sure I'd be headed to the county lockup.

Shit. How many times had I considered giving up my gig with the private security and intelligence firm? Every time I was this damned tired. The pay was *un-fucking-believable*, but the hours sucked. And like that guy in the movie about the mafia family, whenever I tried to leave, they pulled me back in.

"Hello, Hammer. Are you at your office?" Money asked when he answered my call.

"Negative. I decided to come home first." I wanted to add, "You know, to *sleep*," but I didn't.

"I've just learned they're anticipating asking for a million-dollar bail."

"Just heard that myself."

"Jesus," he muttered, a very un-Money thing to do. "I guess I should come down there and see if I can work something out."

If anything would make his sister's situation worse, it would be for him to show up. Texans didn't take too kindly to interference from outsiders, and he definitely was one. "Uh, no. There will be no working something out, McTiernan. You set foot in this state, and her bail will double. Stay out of it and let me handle it."

"Let me know what you need in terms of funds. I can invoke my power of attorney if necessary. We have them set up for one another."

"Will do, and Money? I meant what I said. *Do not* come down here."

"Understood, Hammer. It's just that, you know, I promised my dad on his deathbed that I'd take care of Maeve. I haven't done a very good job of it."

"I got it covered."

"What about a writ bond?"

I'd already thought of that and said so. It wasn't legal in many states, but in Texas, an attorney could submit a request to the sheriff to set an amount to secure a person's release in advance of their court appearance. It was only temporary. The law required the person to attend a bond-condition hearing within ten days of their arrest, where a judge might set other conditions— such as increasing or decreasing the bail amount.

I should've thought to ask Mac what he'd take as a bond from me while I had him on the phone. Given the greater charge of attempted murder should be dropped, in my opinion, maybe he'd be willing to consider something lower. On the other hand, she shot his brother, and while it was in the leg, a GSW could lead to all kinds of things—including death—depending on where it hit.

In addition to asking about the writ bond, that was the first thing I should've asked Mac—about Bobby's condition—something I would've thought to do if I'd gotten more than a couple of hours of sleep in the last forty-eight.

"Give me a rundown on your sister. What should I know before going in?"

He chuckled. "I'm not sure either of us has time for that." He sighed. "She's my half sister and quite a bit younger than I am. My father married my stepmom a couple of years after my mother died, and Maeve came along ten months later. I was twelve at the time and in boarding school here in the States. Maeve was born in Ireland and lived there until my father passed away three years ago."

"What about her mother?"

"Died when Maeve was five."

That explained a lot. Older father, mom died young. "Any other siblings?"

"Nope. We're it for each other."

"If that's the case, what's she doing in Texas?"

"You got me, Hammer."

"Is there anything else you can tell me?" I refrained from adding the word *useful.*

"If you've talked to Mac, you already know some of it. The most important thing, I suppose, would be that my sister's two least favorite words are 'no' and 'don't.' They're a trigger of sorts for her. Reverse psychology works much better with Maeve. Tell her no, and that's the first thing she's going to rush out and do. Case in point, buying that bar."

"Understood. Anything else?"

"One of the reasons I think she gets away with it is her looks. Dark, almost black hair, striking blue eyes, and perfect features. She looks like her mother and nothing like our dad and me." Money laughed.

I'd never seen this side of the man. Normally, he was all business. Zero emotion. He was extraordinarily intelligent—off the charts, in fact. "Did she get your smarts?"

"She's smart. There's no doubt about it."

"College?"

"Negative."

If I recalled correctly, Money was thirty-six, the youngest CIA director in history. That meant his sister was twenty-four.

"Where'd she get the money to buy the Long Branch?"

"Inheritance. Her mother's family was quite wealthy. If it had been up to me, she wouldn't have gotten a penny until she was at least thirty, but the trust didn't come from my family."

"How much are we talking?"

"Fifty million."

"Whoa." Not the figure I was expecting to hear. Now I understood why Money said he had her power of attorney rather than offer to post the bail himself. It was also the reason the amount was so high.

Beautiful—according to her brother—smart, wealthy, and doesn't like to be told she can't or shouldn't do something. The woman was the walking definition of a flight risk, which didn't bode well for me and the writ bond.

I could afford the hundred grand, if it came down to it, but I'd hunt her down and wring her pretty little neck if she jumped. "What's she want with a bar?"

"No idea. One thing I won't ever profess is that I understand Maeve McTiernan."

Something told me I wouldn't either. While I'd hoped this would be the year I could slow down a little, it was looking like that wasn't going to happen.

2

Maeve

The third *feckin'* day of the year, and I was spending it in jail. If only I hadn't shot Bobby MacIver. Not that he didn't deserve it, the bloody bastard. Thank the good Lord my gun hadn't been pointed somewhere potentially more fatal—like his head.

The rest of the stuff I'd been charged with, well, at the time, none of it seemed like a big deal, but when the sheriff started listing them, it kind of did.

So here I was, sitting in a jail cell. Thankfully alone, but given they warned me it could be more than forty-eight hours before I saw a judge, I doubted my solitude would last.

"McTiernan?" a guard shouted.

Seriously? I was the only one in the cell.

"That's me."

"Let's go."

"Where are you takin' me?"

"You made bail."

"How could I make bail when I haven't seen the judge?"

"Listen, Dublin, you can come with me, or you can stay in jail. Which is it going to be?"

"I'll come with you."

"Thought so."

He unlocked the barred door and motioned for me to go ahead of him. "Hold up," he said when I did what he told me to. "Gotta put these on until we're up front."

The *feckin'* asshole handcuffed me. "Is this really necessary?" After he tightened them a couple more clicks, I thought to keep my mouth shut.

"She's all yours," the guard said to a bald but seriously attractive man standing at the desk.

"I'm your lawyer, Dublin."

"Dublin? First him." I pointed at the guard. "Now you?"

"He started it," said the uniformed man, uncuffing me, then handing me a bag of the personal belongings they'd taken when they brought me in. Except for my gun, of course. "Sign here."

I scrawled my signature. "What now?"

"Come with me." The bald man led me out to the parking lot and over to a Porsche 911 Sport Classic. I knew what model it was because I owned one myself and there were only two hundred and fifty built.

As gentlemanly as good-looking, he held the passenger door open for me. I watched as he closed the door behind me, then walked around the front of the automobile. Stalked was more like it, and what the heck was the deal with the cigar? Did he intend to smoke it in these confined quarters? He'd best not.

"Here's how this is going to go," he began once we were a few minutes into the drive. "Believe me when I say this is not the way I want it, but it's all the sheriff would agree to."

This didn't sound good. "The sheriff?"

"Yep. I posted what's known as a writ bond. Meaning it's my money on the line, Dublin."

"I can pay you back—"

"Not the point. It isn't just my money. It's my ability to do this again in the future, and believe me, I cannot have that jeopardized. Which means you'll do what I say, when I say it. You will make your court appearances and every other thing the judge requires you to do. Based on some of your charges, you're going to be looking at a couple hundred hours of community service."

"Sounds like jail would be a better option," I said under my breath.

"That can be arranged, not that your brother would be too happy if it came down to that."

"I was surprised not to see him standing at the counter instead of you."

"Would've been impossible, considering he's not a lawyer or licensed to practice in Texas."

"He is a lawyer, actually." I looked out the window, realizing I had no idea where we were. "Where are you taking me?"

"My ranch."

"What did you say?"

"You heard me, and there isn't any point in pretending you didn't."

"Why?"

"I already told you. They were the only terms the sheriff would agree to."

"Why?" I repeated.

"Because, Dublin, this here is Texas and the guy you shot is his brother."

"*Feckin'* hell," I mumbled.

"You got that right."

God, this time, I had really made a mess of things. I looked over at the man driving, reaffirming my initial impression of his looks.

He was hot. He had to be well over six feet tall, and while bald, he had a scruff of facial hair. It wasn't quite a beard, but it looked intentional.

Since we left the jail, he'd been wearing dark glasses. I didn't notice the color of his eyes while we were still inside; I'd been too distracted by the man's muscles.

Good Lord, he was built. How did he find dress shirts with arms big enough? His pecs were evident even though he wore an undershirt beneath the starched button-down. Earlier, when we walked to his car, I'd noticed how his waist was tapered, and that arse—God, it filled his trousers perfectly.

"Do you have your clothes tailored?"

"Huh?"

"You know, custom made?"

He laughed. It was deep and hearty, full of strength and power. No doubt everything about the man was.

He pulled up to a gate, and we waited for it to open. When he drove through, I saw cattle on the horizon. "It's an actual *ranch*," I gasped. "How big is it?"

"First lesson when it comes to a man's land"—he cleared his throat—"among other things, is it isn't polite to ask."

"Funny, but seriously, how many acres?"

He shook his head and laughed like he had before but didn't answer my question. Just like he hadn't answered when I asked about his clothes.

"Am I permitted to ask about the animals you keep?"

"Livestock—or cattle—and if you did, I wouldn't know enough to answer."

"You have livestock you know nothing about?"

"Bought the ranch. Came with cattle and someone to run it, but he didn't last too long."

"No?"

He shook his head and laughed again. "Not even a week. Hired another guy, though."

"I sense there's a story there, Texas. Or should I call you Drip, seeing that's where you live?"

"You're funny."

"I don't have much choice since I've no idea what your name actually is."

"Shit, I gotta get some sleep." He rubbed the top of his head. "I apologize. Name's Sterling Anderson, but most everyone calls me Hammer."

"You aren't serious?"

He laughed again. And didn't answer.

We went around a bend, and he pulled up in front of what I suppose could be called a house. Without a word, he got out of the Porsche, walked to my side of the car, opened my door, and motioned to the entry.

"You aren't serious!" I repeated. "This is where I'm staying?"

"It's where we're staying."

"Wait. This is *your* house?" The thing looked like a strong breeze would level it.

"That's right." He opened the front door and waved me in. While it appeared clean, the inside was even more appalling than the exterior. "You're a seemingly successful attorney with a 'big' ranch, and this is where you live?"

"For now."

"Take me back to the jail if you'd like, but I am *not* staying here."

He took ten steps to the back of the place, then returned with a pillow and a blanket. He tossed both on the settee. "Sure, you are. There's your bed."

3

Hammer

I wasn't really going to make her sleep on the couch. If I was, I wouldn't have given her my favorite pillow. It was fun to see her squirm, though. I'd managed it a couple of times on our drive here.

I wondered if she realized how hard I was trying not to use the words "no" or "don't." Maybe not yet, but I guessed she'd eventually pick up on it.

"I've been out of town, so I don't have much to eat here. Are you hungry now, or can you wait until later?"

"I've lost my appetite."

I didn't miss the fact that her eyes perused the living room when she said it.

"When you are hungry, what do you like to eat?"

"I'm a vegan."

I laughed. I didn't do that often, but I sure had in the last hour. "The hell, you are."

"What makes you think I'm not?"

"No vegan would buy the Branch. It's world-renowned for its T-bones."

"Maybe I plan to revise the menu."

"Nah, you're smarter than that."

"You don't know me well enough to be able to tell."

"Wrong. Your brother said you are, and he's the smartest guy I know. I doubt he says that about many people." I pushed the pillow and blanket aside and sat on the couch. "Have a seat." I motioned to one of two chairs. "And you can wipe that look off your face. If you were really as snooty as you're acting, no way you would've bought my favorite bar."

"I haven't bought it."

"Yet."

She shook her head. "I doubt I'd be able to now."

"You never know."

"Some of the charges against me are felonies."

I'd wondered if she realized they were. Obviously, the attempted-murder charge was. "We can probably get them reduced. Or even thrown out."

She put her elbow on her knee and rested her head in her hand. "I've lost interest."

"That easy, huh?"

"If it isn't meant to be…"

"I wouldn't have pegged you as a quitter."

"There's a difference between quitting and getting bored." She looked over at the kitchen. "You really don't have any food in the house?"

"Nothing a vegan would eat."

She smirked at me. "What do you have, then?"

I got up and opened the fridge. Pretty much nothing. A jar of salsa, some questionable eggs, and a couple of beers. "Want a brewski?"

"That would be appropriate if I was thirsty."

"Yeah, but beer fills you up, at least while you're waiting for more food."

"Is there 'more' food?"

"Not so much."

Maeve laughed. "Then sure, I'll have a *brewski*."

By the time I polished mine off, Maeve was stretched out on my couch, hugging my pillow, sound asleep. Her beer sat on the coffee table, still half full. Rather than risk waking her, I went outside to call my ranch manager.

"Hey, Rip."

"Hey, Hammer. Heard you were back. Also heard you weren't alone."

I laughed. "You don't miss much, do ya?"

"Trained not to."

Like me, Zane "Rip" Kailor was a former Marine Raider. He'd been freelancing for the Invincibles for a couple of years but also had experience ranching. When I was forced to fire the previous manager, I reached out to Rip to fill in temporarily. Instead, he asked if he could take it on full-time. In order to accommodate him, I had my contractor finish up a place for him to live first, so he could reside right here on the ranch I hadn't named yet.

"Anything I need to know about the cattle operation, Rip?"

"Woulda heard from me if there was, sir."

I chuckled. "I need to talk to you about my houseguest."

"Go ahead."

"Better if we meet."

"Want me to come to you?"

"Yeah. Can't let this one outta my sight."

"I'm five from you now."

I ended the call and looked out at the horizon. From here, I could see the roof of my new house. Someone would have to know what they were looking for to realize what it was. Why, suddenly, was I anxious for it to be ready to move into? Because of the girl from Dublin sleeping on my couch? Did I really give a shit whether she approved of where I lived? She'd be with me forty-eight hours, tops. Once she went in front of the judge, I'd be off MacIver's hook for being her babysitter.

I hadn't expected Rip to show up on horseback, but it didn't surprise me when he did. I knew being able to ride out every day was one of the reasons he took this gig. That I was aware of his "side work" was another. If the Invincibles gave him an assignment, I'd probably know before he did.

"Where's Maeve?" he asked, dismounting and tying his horse, Jack—short for jackrabbit—to the post near my car.

I put my hands on my hips and glared at him.

"What? I told you I heard you weren't alone."

"Why don't you fill me in on what else you know, so I don't waste my breath."

"McTiernan's half sister. Shot Bobby MacIver, but that's only a fraction of the trouble she's in."

"That about covers it."

"She still wanna buy the Branch?"

"She says no, but I don't believe her."

Rip nodded, looked in the direction of the house, and his eyes scrunched. "I've seen her there."

The idea that he had, irritated me. "And?"

"I don't need to tell you she's one fine-lookin' woman."

Hot as hell is what she was. And beautiful. Money was right about her bright-blue eyes. They were as haunting as they were mesmerizing. And that hair, so black it was almost blue. I wanted to wrap it around my hand and give it a good yank so I could get my mouth on her lips. The expression wasn't as common as it used to be, but her body was the epitome of a brick house—voluptuous yet fit, big tits, a nice round ass, and a waist I could wrap my hands around.

Rip laughed and kicked the dirt with his square-toes. "Yeah, you noticed."

"Fuck off," I muttered under my breath.

The front door opened, and the woman herself walked out. I didn't doubt Rip was thinking the same things I was. A white thermal Henley that looked a size too small was tucked into her low-slung jeans. There was no rodeo buckle on her weaved brown leather belt that matched her square-toes, but I could envision her wearing one.

I shook my head and chuckled.

"Are you laughing at me, Drip?"

"Drip?" I heard Rip mutter.

I pointed in his direction but didn't look at him. "Shut it." That only made him laugh.

"What's so funny?" she asked once she was close enough that I could reach out and run my finger over the swell of her breast peeking out of her white thermal. Not that I did.

I chuckled again. "Nothin'."

"*Feckin' eejits*, both of you." She spun on her heel to go back in the house, but I reached out and caught the belt loop on the back of her jeans before she could.

"Get back here, Dublin. I was just thinkin' all you need to complete this getup is a big ol' buckle."

She spun around and looked me up and down. "You're making fun of what *I'm* wearing?"

"Hang on. I'm not making fun of anything."

"What, then?"

"Can't quite see you barrel racing. More like saddle broncs."

She shook her head and raised a brow, leveling those blue eyes on me but, this time, with a twinkle. "Barebacks for me. What about you, Drip, ever ridden without a saddle?"

Rip choked on his laugh.

I looked over my opposite shoulder and let out a sigh. Better that than saying what I pictured when I thought about her and going bareback.

"You look familiar," I heard her say to my ranch manager. "Where do I know you from?"

"Might've shared a dance or two over at the Branch."

"That's it." She looked him up and down like she had me but appeared to like how he looked better. "You're a good dancer."

Rip tipped his hat. "Thank you, ma'am. Headin' there tonight if you feel like havin' another."

I studied her, waiting to see how she'd react to going to the bar where—according to the sheriff's report— she'd been arrested for attempted murder less than twenty-four hours ago.

"Maybe some other time," she said, looking from him to me. "My beer got warm. I'm going to grab another if that's okay."

"Help yourself."

"Damn," Rip mumbled as she sashayed her hips back toward the house.

"Shut it," I repeated. "While you're at it, shut your damn eyes."

"Are you really making her stay here?"

"Haven't had time to move into the big house."

"She could stay with me." Rip didn't finish his sentence before he lost it. "You should see your face right now," he said once he'd stopped laughing long enough to speak.

"Fuck off," I muttered for the second time.

"I could have the guys pull your furniture out of the barn where it's stored if you want."

"She isn't going to be here that long."

"You sure about that?"

I looked over at him. "You're walkin' a fine line, kid."

He smiled like I was. "Maybe it's time you moved in there anyway."

"I'll think about it."

"I was at the Branch last night, you know."

My eyes bored into his. "Why the hell didn't you lead with that? Did you see anything I need to know?"

"Something definitely went down between Bobby and her, but I don't think he was innocent in all this."

"You don't *think*?"

"She was sittin' at the bar, and he was behind it. Pretty soon, the two disappeared into the back. Alone."

I didn't like the sound of this. "Where exactly?" I knew Rip well enough to realize that if he saw that much, he'd made it his business to keep watching.

"Into his office. He was up to somethin'. I knew as much when he looked around before closing the door behind him."

"I take it he didn't see you."

"Hell no, Hammer."

"What happened next?"

"They were in there two or three minutes—give or take—when I heard the gunshot."

"Were you the first person on the scene?"

"I was, and I'll tell you, Maeve looked mighty unsettled."

"Come on, what does that even mean?"

"I don't think she meant to shoot him."

"That isn't the way Bobby tells it."

"There's more to it, Hammer. I'm certain of it."

"All right. I'll see if I can get her side of it. Why'd you ask her if she wanted to go back there tonight?"

"Wanted to know how she'd react."

That made sense, and now that I knew his concerns, I understood why he'd done it. I also understood why Maeve might have kept her mouth shut about what really went down, given Mac was the first law enforcement to arrive. At least, that's what the report the deputy gave me said.

"Was there anything else, boss?"

"The terms of her release were that I keep my eye on her until a hearing can get on the docket. It's the only way Mac would release her."

"And you want me on standby in case one of the boys needs you."

Yep, that was exactly what I needed because when someone from the Invincible Intelligence and Security Group called, I usually had to head out as soon as I could. Sometimes, they gave me as long as a couple of hours to get my shit together. Most often, it was less.

Rip nodded, untied his horse, and threw a leg over. "You know where to find me."

"Hold up a sec," I said before he could ride off. "Might be a good idea to get that furniture out of the barn."

"You got it. I'll have Misty pick up some sheets and stuff too."

Misty was my housekeeper, not that she'd had too much to do in the old house. "If she's going out, maybe have her pick up some food too."

"I'll take care of it."

"And some beer."

"You know it." He flicked the brim of his hat and rode off.

4

Maeve

What in the bloody hell had I done? So *feckin'* stupid. Not only had I landed my arse in jail, but now I doubted I'd ever be able to set foot in—let alone buy—the place I'd given up my life in Ireland for. It wasn't the reason I came to America, but it became the reason I wanted to stay.

Sure, there were times when the Long Branch felt more like a barn than a bar, but that was one of the reasons I loved it enough to impulsively decide to buy it the minute I heard it was for sale.

Even though it was out in the middle of nowhere, the place was the size of the more famous cowboy bar just north of Houston. And like the other place, it had a full-service restaurant and live music. To some, it might seem like a crazy place for me to land, but it felt right to me, and that was all that mattered.

Now, it would probably never come to be, all because the arsehole who owned it had to go and ruin everything.

When Bobby—the *feckin' eejit*—told me he wanted more money for it, I was so bloody angry. The first thing I thought was that he'd found out I had the money, so he thought to take advantage. What happened next, though, was why I'd shot him.

"Sorry if we woke you," said Hammer, coming in the door.

I glanced over my shoulder. "You didn't."

"You must be starving."

"Like you said, beer fills the stomach. At least temporarily."

"Maeve?"

I sighed, still staring out the window over the kitchen sink, wishing I had a few more minutes to get myself together before I had to turn around and look at him.

The man *unnerved* me. He wasn't just so hot he made my blood boil with desire; he was also quick-witted. My weakness.

I gave him another over-the-shoulder glance. "Yeah?"

"There's something I'd like to talk to you about."

"Okay."

"It would be nice to be able to look at you while I'm doing it."

I took a deep breath and turned my body to face him. "Most people consider my arse my better side." As long as I could keep the waggish barbs coming, maybe he wouldn't rattle me so much.

"Rip was at the Long Branch last night."

I nodded, doing my best not to react. "Is he a witness, then?"

"The way he told it, there were no witnesses."

"Does that truly change anything? I did shoot him."

"He seems to think there was more to it than that."

My eyes met his, and as much as I wanted to tear them away, I couldn't.

"Listen, I'm not just the guy who got you out on bail. I'm here to help you."

"I may be beyond help."

He took two steps closer, but with the counter behind me, I couldn't step back.

"You'll get through this, Dublin."

I smiled, of course. How did he do that? In one breath, we were talking about me shooting a man, and the next, he was back to unnerving me.

"First things first, and that's to get the attempted-murder charge dropped. To do that, you're going to have to be honest with me about what really happened."

While on the one hand my brother had called this man to help me, on the other, this was Texas, as he'd said. I had no idea whether it was truly safe to trust him. Until I was sure, I'd not tell him or anyone else what had really happened.

"Maeve?"

I raised my head, realizing he was still talking. "Sorry, what?"

"I said the rest of the charges aren't as serious. They wouldn't have been at all if you'd taken care of them at the appropriate time."

Lecturing. That's what he was doing, and I hated it. And yet, between that and not knowing whether he was trustworthy, I still wanted my hands on him. And his on me.

"Anyway, I gotta eat."

I shook my head. "What did you say?"

"I'm starving, and another beer isn't gonna cut it. Come on, let's go."

I followed him out to the Porsche, happy to be able to watch his arse rather than him, mine. And happier that we were finally going to get some food.

"So, you want a salad?" he asked once we were both in the car.

I burst out laughing. "I *detest* salad."

"You don't know how relieved I am to hear that."

When he opened the engine up once we were on the road, it made me wish I was the one driving. I closed my eyes and rested my head against the seat, loving the four hundred horses that made this baby move.

"Listen, I'm not going to keep bringing this up, but do you have a permit for the gun you shot him with?"

I opened my eyes and looked over at him. "Of course I do. That doesn't change the fact that I took it into a bar."

He nodded but, otherwise, didn't appear to be waiting for me to say anything else, so I closed my eyes again.

When we came to a hard stop, I woke with a start, stunned that I'd fallen asleep a second time in the last hour.

"Sorry," I mumbled.

"Don't apologize. I'm sure you didn't sleep much last night."

"Not at all, actually."

"I'm not surprised. Let's get you fed, and we'll head back."

"Oh!" I squealed, clapping my hands when I realized he'd parked in front of my favorite barbecue joint. "I love this place." I was especially happy, given I felt like I hadn't eaten in days. Probably because I couldn't remember the last time I had.

One of my favorite things about this restaurant was that the menu changed daily. The owners wrote the day's offerings on a blackboard, and there weren't many options. Today, though, I'd probably order one of everything.

"Hey, Maeve, Hammer," said Billy when we walked in. He and his wife owned B & A BBQ. "I didn't know you knew each other." He looked out the window. "Wait. Whose car is that?"

"Mine. You know that," Hammer responded.

When Billy looked at me, I gave a slight shake of my head.

"Yeah, what was I thinkin'? So, what can I get y'all today?"

"Know what you want yet?"

He might think I'd lost my mind, but did I care? I was ready to jump over the counter and eat whatever I could get my hands on. "I do. I'll have the combo with brisket, ribs, and half chicken."

Billy raised his eyebrows. "You want some sides to go along with that?"

"Definitely. Coleslaw, beans, and girlfriend fries." I turned to Hammer. "If you want some, you'll have to get your own." It was an order and a half, and the menu read, "Cuz she always says she doesn't want any and eats half of yours."

"You want anything?" Billy asked Hammer.

"Same."

"I was joking. You two aren't gonna share?"

"Hell no," Hammer answered before I could. "I'll take Coke in the bottle too."

"Same for me."

Billy laughed but rung us up. When I pulled the cash from my bra and started to count off bills, Hammer put his hand on mine. The heat from it almost made me jerk away.

"You okay?" he asked when I looked down at where it still rested on mine, then up into his eyes.

"I'm fine." I rolled my shoulders and moved out of his reach. "Just really hungry."

"Let me get this."

"No, really, it's fine. I can get my own."

"Dublin?"

"What?"

"Let me buy you lunch, or should I say enough food to feed the two of us for the rest of the week?" He winked.

"Thanks. Next one's on me."

"Not a chance."

"You're one of those, eh?"

"A gentleman? I'd like to think so. My mama would too."

"Have a seat, y'all, and I'll bring your food over when it's ready."

I put my hands on the counter, jumped up so I could reach the man's cheek, and kissed it. "Thanks, Billy."

"You're welcome, darlin'."

"Hey, where's Alicia?" Hammer asked.

"Hey, sweetheart, you back there?" Billy shouted behind him.

"You know I am. What do y'all need?"

"Hammer's gettin' nervous I'm gonna steal his girl."

Alicia poked her head through the opening between the counter and the kitchen. "His girl? Is that Maeve?"

She came out from the kitchen, wiping her hands on a towel. "Get over here, sweetie, and give me a hug. Haven't seen you in a couple of weeks." I fell into her embrace, not wanting to let go. "I heard you got into some trouble last night over at the Branch," she whispered.

I shrugged, but before I could say anything, Hammer did.

"I'm working on getting the charges dismissed."

I raised a brow, wondering if he really was or if he was just saying it for Billy's and Alicia's benefit.

"I'm so glad to hear it. We miss seein' you around here." Alicia patted my cheek. "I gotta get your order together. Y'all go take a seat now."

Before I could walk away, Alicia grabbed my arm. "Are you and Hammer really a thing?"

"No. He's a friend of my brother's."

She fanned herself. "Too bad because that man is fine."

"I heard that," said Billy.

"Don't worry, sugar. He's not as fine as you." Alicia winked and walked into the kitchen.

"Your brother's friend, huh?"

"Isn't that what you are?"

"It isn't all I am."

He tipped back his bottle of Coke when Billy brought them to the table. "God, I love this stuff, and I can't imagine there is *anything* worse for you."

"It looks like you can afford the added calories."

"Why, thank you. You look pretty good yourself." He downed the rest of the bottle but didn't take his eyes off me. And I didn't blink.

5

Hammer

Maybe I should take Rip up on his offer to let Maeve stay with him. Either way, I wouldn't be getting much sleep—and I sure as hell needed it. If she was in my house, that wouldn't be happening. Instead, I'd toss and turn, wishing I was in bed with her rather than on my couch. If she stayed with Rip, I'd probably sit up all night, wondering if he'd crawled into her bed.

Fuck, I was screwed. What I should do is recuse myself, call Money, and tell him I couldn't be trusted with his *little* sister. I tried to imagine her as a youngster, thinking it might turn me off. No luck. I couldn't picture her any different than she looked right now, and that was nothing like a kid.

Then she made it worse by eating with her fingers. *Barbecue.* Which meant with every bite, she licked them.

"Is everything all right?" she asked.

"Fine. Why?"

"You're not eating."

"The Coke might've upset my stomach a little."

She ripped a piece of pork off the rib with her teeth and licked her fingers *again*. "My mum always said it was supposed to settle your stomach." She dropped the rib on the paper-covered tray.

"What happened?"

She looked at me with wide eyes. "I had a memory of my mum."

"Doesn't happen very often?"

"It never happens. Literally. Never."

I studied her, unsure of what to say, but worried that she'd stopped eating.

"I think I need a whiskey."

When I got up to order one, I bumped my tray and sent my "girlfriend" fries flying onto hers.

She picked up a piece of brisket and brought it to her lips. "I'm good on fries, but thanks," she said before putting the meat in her mouth.

When I couldn't think of a witty comeback, I chuckled, shook my head, and walked over to the register. Before I could say anything, Billy handed me a glass with what looked like two fingers of whiskey, neat.

"This is the way she prefers it. What can I get you? Beer?" He walked over to the tap.

"No, thanks. I'm driving."

Billy cocked his head.

"What? I already had one at home."

He shrugged a shoulder, and I took Maeve her glass. "Seems he knows how you like it."

"I guess you could say I'm a bit of a regular."

"I am too. I'm surprised I haven't seen you here before."

"Maybe you have."

I shook my head. "No. I'd remember."

"You would? Why?"

I leaned forward and rested my forearms against the edge of the table. "Because I never would've forgotten someone as beautiful as you."

She smiled, and I saw dimples I hadn't noticed before. "I would've remembered you too."

I pretended to brush my hair away from my shoulder and batted my eyes. "I get that a lot."

I wasn't surprised that both Maeve and I only ate about a quarter of our meal. I probably would've eaten more, but I spent the majority of the time watching her.

Billy packed it all up, and Alicia came out to give each of us a hug goodbye.

"She's out of your league, you know," she said, elbowing me.

"Don't I know it."

Maeve was quiet on the way back to the ranch. In fact, I thought she'd fallen asleep, but then I heard her humming.

"What's that?" I asked.

"Hmm?"

"You're humming."

"I don't really know. It's just in my head sometimes."

"Maybe it's something you heard your mother sing?"

"I hadn't thought of that. You may be right."

When I drove in and parked, she folded her arms.

"You drive a car that cost a quarter of a million dollars new and has only appreciated in value, and yet, *this* is your *house*."

Interesting that she knew that much about my car. "It isn't, actually. I mean it is, but only temporarily."

"While *I'm* staying with you?"

I laughed. "While my other house is being built."

"Oh."

"Would you like to see it?"

"Does it look anything like this one?"

"Nothing like it."

"Then, yes. I would love to see it."

I pulled up to the porte cochere, surprised to see the place lit up.

Maeve's mouth hung open. "Wow."

"Yeah, it's pretty big."

"It's *feckin' huge*."

"Just four bedrooms."

"And what else? Because this place looks big enough to have twenty?"

"Easier to show you." I opened the door and motioned for her to go in front of me.

Once inside, rather than focusing on the terra-cotta-colored flagstone entryway or the rough-wood beams, molding, and doors, all I could see was how out of place the furniture Rip and the guys had moved in looked. Every piece was far too small for the large rooms with lots of light and high ceilings.

Based on the puzzled look on Maeve's face, she held the same opinion. "It's lovely," she murmured. When our eyes met, we both burst out laughing.

"It looked so much better empty."

"It would, wouldn't it?"

She walked into the room on the right, a formal living room with a fireplace along with shelves and wood beams that matched what was in the entryway. Double French doors opened to an outdoor patio.

"You know what would work well here?"

I laughed. "Clearly, I don't."

She smiled with those heart-stopping dimples. "A grand piano."

"Do you play?"

"My mum did, but once she passed, I stopped." She waved her arm and changed the subject back to my *decor*, if you could call it that.

"And by the fireplace, two settees, with a large table between them. Something really grand. And, um, bigger."

I was intrigued. "What else?"

"Large area rugs to define the individual spaces." She walked over to the windows that flanked the French doors. "While you don't want to cover these, some floor-to-ceiling draperies would do well to add drama, but you'd keep them tied back the majority of the time."

"You're good at this."

When she turned, she looked at me like I had three heads. "I'm not, actually. I abhor things like this."

She stalked out of the room, and my heart sank. Why had I opened my big mouth? I followed her into the foyer.

"Look, I'm sorry. I didn't mean to snap at you, but my parents lived a simple life. While my mum's family was fantastically rich, my father's was not. When I was forced to visit my grandfather and his second wife—and that's what it was, being forced— their life was more like *this*." She turned in a circle, motioning with her arms. "And before you say it, I know I sound like a right hypocrite after criticizing your other...um...*house*."

When I laughed again, she did too.

"I'm not making any sense, am I?"

"No, you are."

"It's just that I've always rebelled against the trappings of wealth, and yet, I am the very byproduct of having money, aren't I?"

"I was surprised you knew as much as you did about my car."

A pained expression came over her face. "I wish I didn't have to admit this, especially now, but I own one too."

"I see." Billy's question about whose car was parked out front made a lot more sense. The model was only offered in one color, so it probably looked exactly like hers.

"See? God, I'm such a hypocrite."

I took her hand and pulled her back into the other room. "Finish telling me what you think I should do in here. You can just tell me how wrong I got it. *Please*."

Maeve dropped my hand and put hers on her hips. "A chair there, near the piano. Otherwise, a couple of floor lamps and you're done."

"Sounds good. What about this one?" I led her to the room off the other side of the entry. It was a formal dining room, and the table and chairs that were in it looked like a children's play set in the massive space.

"Easy. A much larger table. That would be all it needs."

"Could I move that table in here?" I asked when we went into the kitchen and over to what I referred to as a breakfast nook, not that I'd tell her that. It probably had a more sophisticated name.

"That could work. You'd have to see it in here." She left the room, and I followed.

"Wait, let me get that," I said when she picked up one of the dining chairs.

"I'm capable, Drip. You get the table." She winked, and I smiled.

"Yes, ma'am."

Thankfully, the set looked okay in the smaller space. At least, I thought it did. When she studied it from different angles, then nodded, I was surprised at my relief. It wasn't that I couldn't afford more furniture. I just found myself wanting her approval.

"The bed is the right size," she commented when we walked through the rooms upstairs.

"Although the rest isn't." Like the furniture downstairs, the side tables and dressers looked tiny.

She walked farther into the suite but didn't respond until she reached the closet. "Oh my God, is this all for you?"

The space was probably bigger than the entire house I was living in presently. "I doubt my stuff would take up a quarter of it."

"Thank God for that."

"Why?"

"Again, I sound like such a bitch, but I could never respect a man who had enough clothes to fill this space."

"What about a woman?"

"Her either."

"I was thinking since Rip had some of the furniture moved over here, we could stay here tonight."

Based on the look on her face, she didn't agree.

"Or not."

"What? No, it's fine."

"What's the look, then, Dublin?"

"Nothing."

I shook my head and folded my arms. "Come on, tell me."

She laughed out loud. "It's just…you said, 'some of the furniture.'"

It took me a minute to figure out what she meant, then I laughed again too. "Oh, you're afraid there's more."

"Sorry."

"Stop apologizing. You aren't hurting my feelings. I'm a lawyer, remember?"

"Lawyers don't have feelings?"

I scrunched my eyes. "No, lawyers aren't interior decorators," I teased.

"This, I love," Maeve said when we walked outside and she saw the fire pit surrounded by Adirondack chairs.

"Looks like it'll be the perfect night to light it up."

When she rubbed her arms, I realized she didn't have any clothes other than what she was wearing. "Can I give you a lift to your place?"

Her eyes opened wide. "Aren't I required to stay here until my hearing?"

"I thought you might like to pick up a few things."

"Oh. Right. Yes, I'd love that."

"Where to?" I asked once we were about to get in the Porsche. "By the way, where is your car?"

"At home. I don't drive it to the Branch."

It wasn't the kind of place someone could catch a car service to. "How do you get there?"

"I also have a 1972 F-100. Beat to hell, but it serves the purpose."

"You know a lot about cars."

"My da loved them. If he'd been the type to blow money, that's what he would've spent it on."

"Wanna drive?"

Her eyes twinkled, but she shook her head. "That's okay."

I tossed her the keys anyway, and she caught them.

"I'm surprised you'll let anyone else behind the wheel."

"I don't." I rubbed the top of my head before getting in the passenger side, trying to assure myself that Maeve knew how to drive a car like this one. At least I hoped so.

On our forty-five-minute drive, I learned she knew how to drive it, all right. Better than I did.

"This is it," she said, stopping in front of a Scandinavian-style home in the tony Hyde Park part of Central Austin.

"It suits you," I commented, taking in the large windows that spanned the entire front of the house. Even the front door was made of glass. Unlike what Maeve had suggested for my place, the window coverings on these were closed.

"I paid far too much for it, but I fell in love with this part of Austin." She turned into the driveway, pulled all the way to the back, and cut the engine.

"Make yourself comfortable. I'll just be a minute." She pointed at a couch once we were inside.

Rather than sit, I looked around. The room could be right out of a magazine. It was modern and sleek, nothing out of place, and perfectly decorated. Even I could recognize that. The art adorning the walls was contemporary and oversized, ideally filling the spaces where each piece hung.

While the kitchen was small compared to the one in my new house, right across the hall from it was a walk-in pantry that looked big enough to have been a bedroom.

"I'm never here," she said, joining me and perhaps feeling as though she had to explain why no matter where I looked, it was spotless. "I love it, though."

"I can see why." If I hadn't been anxious to get out of the city, I would've loved to own a house like this too. "I know you said you don't like decorating, but this place looks spectacular."

"I can't take credit. It came with all the furnishings. I, uh, wasn't sure what I should wear…" She motioned to the different clothes she had on as well as to a garment bag and rolling carry-on. "I don't suppose I can take my car."

I shook my head. "No, but I'm hoping you'll get in front of a judge tomorrow." I'd prefer to talk to Mac about dropping the attempted-murder charge before she did, but I also understood she wouldn't want to wait another twenty-four hours.

"I'd like to stop by the, uh, other house first, so I can pick up a few things," I said once we'd returned to the ranch.

"Sorry, which way? I wasn't paying attention."

"Take a left when you get to the top of the hill." When we crested the rise, my new house was in full view.

"I don't remember seeing this earlier," she said, putting the Porsche in park and climbing out. "It's spectacular."

"I stood on this very spot and decided that's where I wanted to build. As far as not seeing it earlier, we went a different way."

"You said you didn't know anything about livestock. Why did you buy a ranch?"

"Why are you buying a bar?"

"I'm being serious."

"It was something my grandfather always said. 'At the end of the day, there's nothin' more valuable than owning dirt. The more of it a man has, the more he's to be respected.'"

"Interesting premise. Although owning land has been a way to accumulate wealth since the beginning of time."

"He died when I was a kid, but if he were alive today, I'd ask if that's what he really meant. I know it's what my dad believed."

6

Maeve

I studied Hammer's profile as he surveyed his land and the home he'd built on it. While vastly different than mine, if I ever were to live on a large piece of property, I could envision myself wanting something similar. I'd say half its size, but I understood why it had been constructed the way it was—resale. It was what real estate was all about.

He'd been in a daze, but came out of it when his mobile rang.

"Mac, what can I do for you?"

I couldn't hear what the sheriff said, but Hammer's face broke into a smile.

"I appreciate this." He ended the call.

"What?" I said when his expression grew more serious as he walked toward me.

"Mac set up a meeting between Bobby and you."

"Oh."

"This is a good thing. If Mac believed his brother intended to press the attempted-murder charge, it wouldn't be happening."

"What's the purpose?"

"My guess is he expects you to apologize, then he'll tell you what he wants in exchange for dropping it."

"He'll expect me to *apologize*?" No *feckin'* way in hell would I be doing that. I clenched my fists and stalked off.

"Hey, wait! Where are you going?"

I walked down the road he'd told me to turn on, knowing that, eventually, I'd come to his place.

"Hey, stop!" he hollered. "We need to talk about this."

I turned around. "Tell him I said no." Bobby would know exactly why. In fact, it was probably what he expected.

Hammer caught up with me and grabbed my arm. "Tell me what's going on."

"I'll not apologize."

He dropped his hand and shook his head. "What am I missing here?"

"Not a thing,"

When I started walking again, he picked me up and put me over his shoulder.

"Put me down, you *feckin' eejit*!" I shouted, pounding his back with my fists.

"I'm not leaving my car out here for one of the bulls to put a dent in with his horn, and I'm not letting you out of my sight, because that was the promise I made. Since you refused to stop and tell me what the hell is going on, I'm putting you in the car."

By the time he said those words, we were back to the Porsche. He set me on my feet, opened the passenger door, and waved me inside.

"If you even think about getting out of this car until I say you can, I'll take you straight back to jail."

He sounded so much like my brother, I cringed. My da rarely said a cross word to me. Kellen, on the other hand, never held back. Just like Hammer did just now, he would seethe more than shout. That's when I knew I was really in for it.

"When we get to the house, I'll be going inside to grab a few things. It will take me less time than it took you to do the same thing. When I come out, you'll still be in this car, waiting for me. At that point, we'll drive to the new house, and you can tell me what happened when you and Bobby went into that office alone."

I folded my arms and looked out the side window.

"Maeve?"

"All right. I'll stay put."

He was in and out in under five minutes, carrying a small bag, which he put in the boot.

"Who told you?" I asked.

"Rip."

Now I remembered why he looked so familiar. He was the first to come in the office door after I'd shot Bobby and unlocked it.

Hammer didn't speak when we arrived and went inside. Instead, he put the bag he'd brought from the other house on the kitchen counter and pulled out a bottle of bourbon and two glasses. He set those on the counter and poured us each a double shot.

"Drink this." He pushed one in my direction.

I downed it and set the glass on the counter. He poured another.

"I don't want more."

"Then, I'll drink it." He finished what was in both glasses, went out the French door to the patio, and flipped a switch. The fire pit lit up. "Will you be warm enough, sitting out here?"

"Yes."

"Good." He sat and put his feet up on the edge of the stone, then got back up. "Hang on."

I watched him walk from the patio down to his car. I expected he was getting my luggage, but he returned with our leftovers from the barbecue place.

"I'm hungry again." He set one bag in front of me and began removing containers from the other.

When he picked up a piece of brisket and ate it, I couldn't resist doing the same. Ten minutes ago, I wouldn't have thought it possible, but now I felt hungry too.

"The fries suck when they're cold," he said, tossing them back into his bag.

"They do." I hadn't bothered to get mine out. Instead, I was pulling apart pieces of chicken.

"Need a fork?"

"No, thanks. I consider barbecue finger food."

"I noticed."

"Sorry."

"Don't be. I enjoyed it."

I studied him, wondering what he meant, perhaps hoping he'd explain himself, but he kept eating.

"Listen, about—"

"We'll talk after we eat."

I wanted to be irritated with him for interrupting me, but I couldn't help but appreciate his patience.

After taking his time, Hammer sat back in the chair and put his hand on his stomach. "I go from hungry to so full I feel like I'm going to bust a gut. Why can't I ever just end up somewhere in the middle?"

"I'm surprised you don't. You eat quite slow."

"I like to savor every flavor." He wriggled his eyebrows, and I laughed.

I was facing an attempted-murder charge after shooting a man who expected me to apologize for it, something I refused to do, and here I sat—laughing. How was it possible?

Hammer reached over and touched my hand. "We'll talk tomorrow. It's been a long day, and you've got to be exhausted."

"When am I supposed to meet with Bobby?"

"I called Mac and told him it was a no-go."

"But—"

"Until you tell me what happened in that room, I'm not going to force you to talk to him. I wouldn't force you anyway, but in my head, saying that sounded better than saying I wasn't going to allow you."

Again, I smiled. "You're a good man, Drip."

"That means a lot, coming from you, Dublin."

"I want to tell you. Tonight, I mean."

"Are you sure you're ready?"

I nodded. "Be right back." If I was going to do this, trust him not to be in cahoots with the sheriff and Bobby, I needed some more of that bourbon. Before taking the bottle and two glasses out to the fire pit, I took a long swig, brushed my mouth with the back of my hand, and rolled my shoulders.

I poured two shots for each of us and handed Hammer one of the glasses.

"Am I gonna need this?" he asked.

"I am."

He tossed his back. "I'll pour," he said when I reached for the bottle. "Sit down."

"I can't."

"Okay. Don't." He winked when I took a seat.

"What?"

"Nothin'."

"I need to ask you something."

"Sh—go ahead."

I laughed. "Were you about to say 'shoot'?"

"Yeah." He hung his head and shook it. "What's your question?"

I looked him in the eye. "Can I trust you?"

"I'm your attorney."

"Answer the question."

He didn't flinch. "Yes, Maeve, you can trust me."

"Bobby was drunk."

"That doesn't surprise me. From what I've heard, it was one of the reasons he wanted to sell. The drinking got out of hand."

"He asked me to come back to the office with him, and like a *feckin' eejit,* I went." I motioned to the shot glass, and he poured another.

"How much had you had to drink?"

"That night?"

He nodded.

"A couple of pints."

"Beer?"

I raised a brow.

"Got it. Go on."

"You know I have…money."

"I do. Your brother told me about your inheritance."

"It's a lot of money."

"Fifty million."

"That's what I inherited. Not what I'm worth now."

"More?"

"A lot more." I looked up at the sky. "I've made some good investments."

"Congratulations."

"As you can imagine, having that kind of money attracts the kind of attention a more insecure woman might succumb to."

"But not you."

"Never me." I stood and walked to the other side of the fire. I'd just lied. There'd been one time. Never again, though. "Fuck," I muttered under my breath.

7

Hammer

"We don't have to do this tonight."

"I need to." She stretched one arm over her head, then the other. Next, she twisted at the waist before reaching down and grabbing her ankles. When she stood back up, she shook her whole body. "Sorry. This is really hard for me."

"Why?"

Her eyes scrunched, and her gaze met mine. "Because I don't trust people. Experience has taught me not to."

"Did you trust Bobby?" She looked out into the darkness. That question hit a nerve.

"More than I should have."

"What happened in that office?"

"He told me he changed his mind about selling. It was obvious what he was up to. I asked him how much more he wanted." She smiled. "That's not exactly what I said, but close enough."

"I figured as much."

"*Twice* the original price. I was furious. As you probably also 'figured.'"

"I'm not surprised."

She took a couple of deep breaths and let them out slowly. "He suggested a different deal."

"He put sex on the table."

"When the bastard got up and unfastened his belt, I turned to leave, but not fast enough. He grabbed my arm, and I managed to twist out of his grasp, but again, not fast enough. He grabbed me again."

"And you grabbed your gun."

"Aye." She patted the left side of her waist.

"You're left-handed."

"The one time in my life it proved useful."

"What happened next?"

She pulled up the right sleeve of her sweater. The angry bruises were consistent with the story she told. "When he jerked my arm…I didn't mean to pull the trigger."

As much as I wanted to jump up, pull her into my arms, and comfort her, it would've been too much like what Bobby had done to her that night. "Maeve?"

She wrapped her arms around her waist and looked up at me. "I just wanted him to let me go."

"Of course you did." This is why Mac said it was a case of "he said/she said." He knew something didn't add up.

I held out my hand when her gaze didn't leave mine. "Can you come over here and sit down?"

She nodded but went around the fire in the opposite direction. When she sat, I poured her a healthy shot and handed her the glass. "Drink."

I had a shot myself and processed through everything she'd just told me. Self-defense, definitely. Enough to prosecute Bobby for attempted sexual assault, probably not.

"I'm going to take care of this."

"Don't say it unless you're sure."

"I'm more than sure, Dublin."

She smiled.

I'd been curious about something since I talked to Money. "I have a question."

"Shoot." She winked.

"Why Texas?"

Maeve picked up the nearly empty bottle of bourbon. "That's a question for another bottle, another night."

I studied the woman, who was wise far beyond her years.

"What?" she asked.

"I have a lot of respect for you, Maeve McTiernan."

"That means a lot, coming from you, Drip."

"I say we call it a night." When I stood, she didn't. "Or not."

"Thank you for believing me."

I sat on the edge of the fire pit. "I have no reason not to."

"I *am* tired."

I held out my hand, and this time she took it.

Too tired to argue with me, and maybe a little too drunk, Maeve agreed to sleep in the master bedroom while I took the guest room down the hall. Fortunately, Misty had bought bedding for that room too.

The next morning, I slept much later than I normally would have. Then again, I was making up for lack of rest. When I did get up, the bed she'd slept in was empty. I hated where my mind went, but the first thing I did was look out the window to see if my Porsche was still there. It was, as was Maeve, who was doing yoga on the patio. She wore an oversized sweatshirt over tight black pants and still looked sexier than any other woman I'd ever known.

I was fourteen years her senior. Her brother was only twelve years older. I felt like a lech, but I kept watching anyway. When she stretched her shoulder like she had last night, she looked up and our eyes met. She wiggled her fingers in a wave, and I smiled.

"You should join me," she said when I walked outside a few minutes later with a cup of coffee.

"My body could never get into all those positions."

"Maybe not at first, but gradually."

"You forget how old I am."

"Don't use it as an excuse."

She wiped her forehead with a towel and walked over to sit in the same chair she had last night.

"How long have you been out here?" I asked.

"An hour or so." She looked at her watch. "Actually, closer to two."

I raised a brow. "I guess that bourbon didn't hit you as hard as it hit me."

"No, it did. Yoga helps, though." She closed her eyes and rested her head on the back of the chair. "What happens today?"

"I'd like to set up a meeting with Mac before a court appearance is scheduled."

She sighed.

"John MacIver is a good man. I know you don't trust that he'll do the right thing, but I do."

"Set it up."

"Yes, ma'am."

When she opened her eyes and looked over at me, I winked.

"I'll get ready."

Yeah, I watched her walk away. What man with a pulse wouldn't have? As soon as I was sure she was inside, I called the sheriff.

"Your client have a change of heart?"

"No, Mac, but I think you will."

"What have you got, Hammer?"

"Let's meet."

"I'll come to you. Be there in an hour."

The fact that he offered to, backed up my belief that he was questioning whatever story his brother had told him.

"Come alone, Mac."

"Roger that."

I stayed outside, taking in the crisp January air and enjoying my coffee. Most times, I loved the solitude of being here. When I traveled on behalf of the

Invincibles, I was usually surrounded by people and anxious to get home and away from them. Today, though, I found myself disappointed Maeve wouldn't be sticking around longer.

I heard the door open and watched her walk toward me, much in the same way I'd watched her walk away earlier. "Hi."

"Hey. I talked to Mac." I looked at my watch. "He'll be here in about forty-five minutes."

She sat down and took a sip of coffee. "This is good."

"Special Texan blend. I thought maybe you'd prefer tea."

"Everyone assumes that."

"I'd like to discuss our meeting with the sheriff. Will you feel comfortable telling him what you told me last night? I'll be with you as your attorney, and just so you know, I asked him to come alone."

"Thank you, and yes. Now that I've told it once, I don't think it will be as difficult the second time."

"How about a third time?"

"What do you mean?"

"I'd like you to tell me again before he gets here, so I can make some notes."

Maeve went through the same story she had last night without any inconsistencies. "Can you show me how he grabbed you?"

"Sure."

We stood, and she got herself in position. I remembered approximately where the bruises I saw last night were and tried to avoid them. Maeve moved my hand, though.

"It was more here." She reenacted taking out her gun and the way she'd held it in her hand. At six feet two, Bobby and I were the same height, which meant the position of the gun would be almost identical with me. From what I remembered from the police report, it was in the vicinity of where the bullet hit him.

"Let me ask you one more thing."

"Go ahead."

"Do you still want to buy the Long Branch?"

"I told you before I've grown bored with the idea."

"I don't believe you."

"I haven't decided one way or the other."

"If you do decide you want to, you're going to have to get some of this other stuff taken care of. The good news is the warrants that have been issued are all for misdemeanor violations. Have you started the process of getting a liquor license?"

"You probably won't believe this, but I was going to attempt to get the tickets taken care of this week."

I laughed. "I believe you."

She smirked. "You don't."

"I told you last night I have no reason not to." I got an alert on my phone and answered even though I already knew it was Mac at the gate. "Come on in, Sheriff. We're at the new house." I pressed the code for the entrance to open remotely.

"Ready?"

She shook each arm. "Aye."

Mac was all Texas swagger when he got out of the cruiser and walked in our direction.

"Hey, Mac. Thanks for coming out here."

"Always nice to see the ranch. You name it yet?"

I shook my head. It wasn't a matter of just hanging onto the name it had before I bought it. In this case, I'd bought three different properties and merged them together. No way was I combining all those names.

"Maeve," he said, tipping his hat.

"Sheriff MacIver."

I studied the man I'd known since before I passed the bar. Now that I was paying attention, I realized he looked as though he'd aged a few years in the last couple of months.

"Mac, I'd like you to listen to Maeve's accounting of what happened the night she was arrested."

He nodded and pulled a notepad and pen out of his back pocket.

"Would you prefer to go inside?" I asked.

"Got a place to sit in there? How about a pot of coffee?"

I chuckled and put my hand on his shoulder. "Yes, and you know it."

"See you've made progress. You even have some furniture," he said when we walked into the kitchen and I motioned to the table Maeve and I had moved in from the dining room.

Mac and I waited for her to take a seat, but when she didn't appear she was going to, I asked if she'd mind if we did.

"Oh. Sorry. Of course. Thank you."

I set my friend's coffee on the table and motioned to his chair.

"As you can imagine, the fact that Bobby is your brother makes what Maeve is about to tell you uncomfortable."

"He's been my little brother a helluva long time, Hammer. Can't say he's ever been perfect. Far from it."

"Maeve? You ready?"

She nodded and unbuttoned her sweater. When she shrugged it off her shoulders and her arms were bare, I nearly gasped at the bruises. They looked so much worse than they had last night. Mac hung his head.

I had to admit, it was the best way for her to begin the accounting.

Mac turned to me. "Take photos if you haven't." He looked up at Maeve. "I know we have your intake pictures"—he motioned with his finger—"but those look a lot worse today." I watched him make some notes on his pad.

"Go ahead," I said to Maeve when he looked up at her.

The sheriff and I listened, and she reiterated her story in the exact same way she had to me both times she told it. No detail varied.

"Bobby and I are the same height, Mac. I asked Maeve to show me what happened right before she shot him. We can do that again now, if you'd like."

He shook his head. "Not necessary." He looked from me to her. "Do you want to press charges?"

She looked at me. "It's up to you," I told her.

"I hadn't considered it a possibility."

"Self-defense," Mac muttered.

"Enough for attempted assault?"

"Might not be enough in a courtroom, but to scare some sense into Bobby? Absolutely."

"Maeve?"

Her eyes scrunched, and I stood. "Mac, give us a minute?"

"Of course."

I led her out of the room far enough that I was sure we were out of earshot. "Tell me why you're hesitating."

"The Long Branch."

"Go on. What about it?"

"He won't let me buy it."

I smiled. "The bar you go back and forth whether you want or not."

She smiled too. "The very one."

"I can't make it an official deal."

"I know."

"Unofficial is another story."

Her eyes stayed targeted on mine.

"I need you to trust me, Dublin, but I'll do whatever you want to do. This is your life. You want to press charges against Bobby? I'll support you. You want to walk away from the whole thing? I'll support that too."

"You're a very good lawyer."

"I am. I'm not shy about saying so. But I think we both know this goes beyond that."

"Thank you, Hammer."

"Do you want some time to think it over?"

"The unofficial deal? Would you talk to Mac about it now if I said I didn't want to press charges?"

"I would, but you can't be in the room when I do." I held up my hand. "Which—again—means you'll need to trust me."

8

Maeve

What he was asking had become one of the hardest things for me to do. It didn't use to be, but one man had managed to destroy my faith in humankind. Now, when someone *asked* me to trust them, I bristled.

Hammer had said he believed me because I hadn't given him any reason not to. He hadn't done anything to give me cause not to trust he would represent me—officially or unofficially.

"Okay."

"Okay, what, Dublin?"

"I'll stay out of the room."

"Actually, you'll have to leave it. First, I need you to tell Mac you don't want to press charges *at this time*."

"Won't that make him suspicious?"

He laughed. "Of course it will, but Mac is smart enough to know what's really going on here."

"This kind of thing happens all the time, doesn't it?"

"Not as much as you'd think."

I rolled my shoulders and reached behind with one hand to stretch the muscle. It's where my tension resided, and right now, that part of my body was on fire. I stretched the other side.

Hammer's gaze traveled from my eyes to my breasts before he turned his back to me.

Yes, Drip, I wanted to say. *I want to check you out just as much.* "I'm ready," I said instead.

I followed him back to the room where the sheriff waited.

"Go ahead," said Hammer.

I repeated his words verbatim. "I don't want to press charges at this time."

I thought I saw the briefest grin before the sheriff rested his head in his hand and thereby covered his mouth. "Understood."

"Mac, is there anything else you need to discuss with Ms. McTiernan?"

"Let's chat, Counselor," he responded.

I left the room, went upstairs to the master suite, and shut the door. I lay on the bed and ran my hands over the duvet, knowing Hammer had never slept under it. When I went exploring this morning, long before he was awake, I found evidence the linens had been purchased yesterday. I wished he had, though. To imagine him here, to breathe in his scent, led me to the kind of thoughts I hadn't had in weeks. Months, really. I was astounded yesterday when my libido raised its head. More so now, when I was tempted to put my hand between my legs.

What if I did but left the door open? Would he come upstairs to report on his conversation, and when he found me writhing, join me on his bed?

Earlier, I'd thought about wearing the one dress I brought with me and go *sans* knickers. Chickening out, I wore trousers instead.

I rolled to my back, unable to keep my hand from pressing against my pussy, relieving the ache, but only momentarily. My fingers found the clasp at my waist, unfastened it, and lowered the zipper. I eased my hands inside until I could feel my own wetness.

How long had it been since I'd *wanted* sex? Now I couldn't stop myself from masturbating. Imagining his fingers, his hands, his mouth, his cock, it took one touch of my clit to bring me to an orgasm so powerful, I cried out.

9

Hammer

"What does she want?" Mac asked.

"To buy the Long Branch for the original price negotiated."

"In exchange for agreeing not to press charges?"

I pulled the cigar case from my pocket. "You know better than that, Sheriff." I took the stogie out and brought it to my nose, inhaling the newly sown fields and rain-soaked earth scent of the unlit cigar.

"You still smokin' those things?" Mac asked.

"Nah. More, I just put it in my mouth like I'm going to, but never light it."

"Those things will kill ya."

I set the cigar on the table and rested my forearms against its edge. "You wanna talk about what's gotten into Bobby? I've known him as long as I've known you, and this kind of shit isn't like him."

"He's goin' through some stuff."

"Seems like more than *stuff*, Mac."

"I hear ya."

"If there's anything I can do," I offered when he didn't elaborate.

"Ain't nothin' nobody can do." As if he'd come out of a trance, Mac's expression changed and he stood. "I'll let Bobby know where he stands."

I stood too. "Heard anything about getting in front of a judge?"

"No, but I expect to. Better be on my way and let the DA know what we've talked about."

"Appreciate it."

"Tell that girl to put the rest of her shit in order so she can get a damn liquor license."

"Will do. Think Bobby will still want to sell?"

He looked at me with a familiar twinkle in his eyes. "If he doesn't, I'll convince him."

After seeing Mac out, I went upstairs in search of Maeve. I was about to knock on the bedroom door when I heard her cry out. It didn't sound like she was in pain.

Lord, how I wanted to crack the door open and peek in. Would she be writhing on the bed I hadn't slept in yet, her fingers between her legs? As I watched, would she put two of her fingers into the place I wanted to bury my now-steel-hard cock?

I rested against the wall outside the door. As much as I longed to feel her naked body against mine, I couldn't. She was my client and the younger sister of a man who trusted me. She trusted me too. If I went into that room, I'd be betraying both of them. Her especially.

I closed my eyes and held in a groan when I heard her moan my name.

I walked down the stairs and outside, silently swearing the entire way. I had to get Maeve the fuck out of my house before I did something I knew I shouldn't.

While not illegal, having sex with her would be immoral. I would have to find her another lawyer if I succumbed to what my cock was trying to get my body to do. And then what? She'd be in the hands of someone *I* didn't trust, and I'd have to explain myself to Money.

I turned toward the house and looked up at the window of the bedroom where she lay, pleasuring the body I wished I could. Maeve stood in the window, face flushed, lust in her eyes. Rather than wave, I walked over to my car, started it up, and took off in the direction of Rip's place.

"Hey, boss," he said, coming out the front door by the time I got out of the Porsche. "Saw Mac drive off a bit ago."

"He's dropping the charge of attempted murder against Maeve."

"Yeah? Did she tell you what went down in that office?"

"She did."

Rip knew better than to ask questions since I didn't offer more details. "When's she leaving?"

"As soon as we can get in front of the judge."

He rested his arms on the crossbeam of the hitching post that stood between us. "That what's got you so rattled?"

"I gotta get out of here for a bit."

"Yeah? Invincibles business?"

I couldn't lie to him. "No. This is personal."

"You want me to head over to the house?"

Did I? Fuck. Half my body wanted him to, and the other half didn't. "Yeah. I'd appreciate it." I stalked back to my car and drove away.

I was almost at Billy and Alicia's place when my phone rang. "Hey, Rip."

"Hammer, you better get back here."

"Why?"

"Bobby MacIver is at the front gate, and from what I can tell, he's damn drunk."

"Call Mac."

"First thing I did. He said to tell you he's on his way. Depending on how far you went, you might be able to beat him here."

"Headed back now."

"Shit," I heard Rip mutter. "See ya when you get here."

The call ended, but whatever made him hang up, obviously needed his attention. I put my foot on the gas when I hit the stretch of road where I knew I wouldn't see anyone else. When the Porsche bumped over one hundred, I eased off the accelerator and let her coast the quarter mile to my ranch.

I pulled up, relieved Mac wasn't there yet. Rip was, and it looked like he and Bobby were about to come to blows.

I pulled inside the gate and spun the car around so it was heading in the opposite direction. I climbed out and stalked over to where the two men were facing off. "What's goin' on here, Bobby?"

"Fuckin' bitch told my brother I attacked her," he slurred.

"Yeah? And why are you here? To finish what you started?"

"It was con-sen-ual—fuck—consensual."

"You and I both know it wasn't."

Before Bobby could say more, Mac pulled up.

"Fuck, man," the younger MacIver cried when his brother put his arm around his shoulders and led him toward the cruiser. "I'm so fucking sorry."

"I know you are," I heard Mac say before he looked over his shoulder. "Either I'll be back or someone else will later to get his truck."

Before Bobby got in the cruiser, he coughed. Mac handed him a handkerchief, and when he put it over his mouth, then pulled it away, it was covered in blood.

"Hey, Mac," I hollered. "Get the keys from him, and Rip and I will deliver it for you," I said without thinking about the ramifications of us both being gone.

Mac did, though. "Did you mean you and Maeve? If so, I don't advise it. I'm taking him home to sleep this one off." He didn't bother to give us the keys, and I didn't ask for them a second time.

"Now what?" Rip asked.

"You can head to your place."

"Roger that."

I watched him pull away before getting in the Porsche. I'd told Rip to go home, but what the fuck was I going to do?

10

Maeve

I wanted to pound my bloody head against the wall. Who was I more mad at? Me, who'd probably made enough noise that Hammer and the sheriff knew exactly what I was doing in the room above where they met? Or Hammer, who I'd trusted and who'd left?

He saw me in the window, and rather than respond to my wave, he got in his vehicle and drove away. Wasn't he supposed to have me in his sight every waking minute? Or had the sheriff already dropped the charges, meaning I was no longer his ward? If that was the case, why hadn't he just taken me home?

I saw the Porsche barreling in this direction. Perhaps the same thing had occurred to him. Would he take me to Austin himself, or would he task Rip with doing so?

Rather than hide out in his bedroom, I went downstairs and into the room right off the foyer. He could hardly miss me there.

When he came in the front door, I stood, arms folded, waiting for an explanation.

"Dublin," he said, rubbing the top of his head with his palm.

"Drip."

"I…uh…had a little emergency to take care of."

The *feckin' eejit* was *lying* to me. He wasn't even attempting to hide it. I knew because I'd studied everything written on the subject, determined not to fall for it ever again in my life. I stormed past him and up the stairs.

"Hey! Where are you going?" he shouted after me.

"Sod off," I said when he followed me into the bedroom before I could shut the door. There was no way in hell I was spending another night in the lying bastard's house.

"What the hell is this all about?"

"I want to go home."

"I understand, but those are not the terms I agreed to in order for you to be released."

"Then, take me back to jail." I threw my clothes into my satchel and was about to zip it closed when he trapped my hands with his.

"Maeve."

"What?" God, I was going to cry. I tried to wriggle my hands free so I could escape to the loo before he saw, but he held tight.

"I'm sorry I left. There really was something I had to take care of, but—"

"Stop," I snapped. "Don't lie—" I turned my head away and shook it. I couldn't continue speaking. If I did, he'd know how fragile I really was. No one could ever know that. Never again.

He moved one of his hands from my wrists up to my chin. With his fingertips, he coaxed me to look at him.

"Talk to me," he pleaded.

"I want to go home." I hated how much I sounded like a child.

"Why?"

"I don't want to be here."

"Why?" he repeated.

Because I trusted you and you lied to me. I raised my chin. "Am I required to remain in your custody?"

"You aren't in my custody." His mobile rang, but he ignored it. When it rang a second time, he swore under his breath and released me.

"Hey, Mac." He paused. "On our way. Thanks." He ended the call and put the phone in his pocket. "Looks like you're going to get your wish. The sheriff has arranged for you to get in front of a judge."

"When?"

"As soon as we can get there."

Before I could pick up my bags, he did. Evidently, he was as ready to get rid of me as I was to leave. The idea of it brought me back to the brink of tears. I walked past him, raced down the stairs, and out to the car.

There was no one in the courtroom when we arrived, but within a few minutes, three people came out from the back at the same time Mac and another man joined us.

"Counselor," said the judge, looking at Hammer.

"Yes, Your Honor?"

"Approach." Both he and the man who'd come in with Mac walked up to the bench.

"This will be over soon," the sheriff said, preventing me from hearing what the other three men were discussing.

"I hope so."

"I want you to know I'm sorry."

I turned to him. His voice sounded more sad than repentant. "You did nothing wrong, Sheriff."

"Call me Mac. All my friends do."

"Is that what we are, Mac? Are we friends?"

"I hope we can be."

"My friends call me Dublin."

I looked over my shoulder and saw Hammer walking toward us. He didn't look happy.

"What's goin' on?" Mac asked. "The DA change his mind?"

"No. Why?"

"You look like someone shot your puppy."

Hammer scowled at him and turned to me. "We'll also be addressing the other charges against you now."

"Okay." I studied him, agreeing with Mac. He looked downright angry. "Is there something you need to tell me?"

Before he could respond, we were called to the podium.

"My understanding is the charge of attempted murder against Ms. McTiernan has been dropped."

"That's right, Your Honor," the DA confirmed.

"What about illegal weapon possession?"

"That stands, Your Honor."

"There are several other charges against you," the judge said, looking directly at me.

"Yes, sir."

He sat back in his chair and steepled his fingers. "Both your lawyer and the district attorney have recommended against jail time."

"Thank you."

"I said 'recommended.' I didn't say I agreed."

"Yes, sir."

The judge turned to Hammer. "You hold the writ bond, is that correct?"

"Yes, Your Honor."

"On the charge of illegal weapon possession, I'm going to impose the maximum fine allowed." He looked back at me. "There is a reason we have these laws, Ms. McTiernan."

"Yes, Your Honor."

He shuffled through some papers, sighed, then removed his glasses. "Are you a United States citizen?"

"I am."

"Naturalized?"

"No, my father was American."

He nodded. "So I can't deport you."

I tried my damnedest not to react.

"The remaining charges against you indicate you hold a disrespect for the law. Why is that?"

"Your Honor," said Hammer.

"Let her answer."

"It isn't as much disrespect, sir, as it is immaturity."

He raised a brow. "You have several fines to pay. Will doing so create a hardship for you?"

"No, sir, not at all." I realized my blunder as soon as I'd said the words. I still had no idea what those fines would be, so how could I say with such certainty? Unless, of course, I had a large disposable income.

"As I suspected." He turned to the woman seated to his left. "Read the remaining charges, please."

As she did, I felt my cheeks burn in embarrassment. He was right to think I felt disrespect. What she read made me sound like a spoiled-rotten child.

He nodded when she reached the end of the list. "What do you have to say for yourself?" he asked.

"Your Honor," Hammer interjected a second time. "May I have a moment to confer with my client?"

"No." The judge waved his finger at me. "You have one chance to get out of this without jail time. Think long and hard before you respond."

"I'm sorry, sir, and I'll not do anything of this kind again," I responded through gritted teeth, trying to keep my temper in check.

"I'll be monitoring you, Ms. McTiernan. If you get as much as a parking ticket, I'll know about it." He looked over at the DA. "Maximum fines on every count along with one hundred community service hours."

The man appeared stunned. "In total, Your Honor?"

"For each count as long as Ms. McTiernan pleads guilty. Otherwise, we can take this to a jury."

"Your Honor," Hammer said for a third time, exasperation evident in his voice.

"You may confer with your client now. Step out." The judge waved his hand in the direction of the door.

"I'm going to suggest you agree to do as the judge stated and plead guilty on all counts," he said after leading me a few feet away from the courtroom.

"Okay."

"It's a lot of community service, and you won't be able to get out of doing it. I can ask for fewer hours, but I doubt the judge will agree."

I also agreed it seemed unlikely. "Time to pay the piper, as they say."

"Maeve, if you do not perform the community service—"

I raised my head and glared at him. "Got it."

When we returned to the courtroom, I listened as the judge reiterated everything he'd already said. As each count was read, I pleaded guilty. At the end, he rattled off dollar amounts along with the already stated one hundred hours of community service per charge. I didn't bother to add up either in my head. I was too distracted by the fact that Hammer and I would soon part company.

"As to the matter of the writ bond. I am convinced Ms. McTiernan still poses a significant flight risk. Until such time as the final hour of community service has been completed, the writ remains intact."

"As opposed to a traditional bond, Your Honor?"

"You heard me, Hammer. The *writ bond* stays in effect until the terms of the sentence are fulfilled. Prior stipulations remain."

The judge banged his gavel, stood, and left the room.

"What does that mean?" I whispered.

Hammer turned to Mac, who shrugged. "To me, it sounds like the terms haven't changed."

"Let's go," he barked.

"I'm sorry about this," I said, trying to keep up as he stalked out of the room, down the corridor, and outside. "I don't know what to do," I added when we got to the car.

"For now, get in."

While his tone made me bristle, I did as he asked.

He was quiet the entire ride back to his ranch, as was I.

Questions raced through my mind. Did this mean I would be required to remain here with him? What about my car? Would I be allowed to drive myself anywhere? What about buying the Long Branch? Would I have to complete my community service before I would be permitted to purchase it?

Hammer pulled up in front of the house and cut the engine. "Before you ask, whatever you're so deep in thought about, so am I."

"Can I go home?"

"I'm not certain, but it didn't sound like it."

"Someone must know."

"I'm sure *someone* does, but until I can talk to the judge's clerk, *I* don't know."

"I'm forced to stay here, then?" I snapped.

"Sorry you find it so unpleasant." Hammer got out of the car and slammed his door. I expected him to go straight inside, but he came around and opened mine. "We need to talk."

11

Hammer

When we arrived at the courthouse, I'd expected two things to happen. First, the attempted-murder charge would be dropped. Second, the writ bond would be discharged. I hadn't expected the judge to address the remaining charges against Maeve, and I sure as hell didn't expect him to say the bond would remain in effect until she completed the terms of her sentence.

This was beyond outlandish. While I hadn't challenged it inside the courtroom, I doubted it was even legal.

Now, though, I needed answers and I intended to get them. We weren't even in the front door when my cell rang with a call from the same man I intended to contact once I finished talking to Maeve.

"Be right back," I said to her. I went upstairs to one of the empty bedrooms and shut the door. "What the ever-loving fuck was *that*?"

Mac laughed. "I'd say ol' Ringer's got you by the balls."

Ringer was what we called Judge Armestus Bell, and he had no reason I was aware of to put me in this position. It wasn't uncommon—particularly in Texas—for judges to step outside of the box of what might be considered standard sentencing and impose either harsher penalties or, in some instances, go more lenient than the district attorney asked for.

"Is this legal?" I asked Mac, somewhat rhetorically.

"As a matter of fact, it is. After you left, I paid a visit to the head honcho over at the DA's office. Seems there's a law on the books dating back to the turn of the century—the one before the last one. I haven't heard of a judge making use of it until now, but then Ringer's up there in years."

"He's not *that* old." Fuck. So the law was on the books, and that meant I was bound by the judge's decree. I could fight it, but by the time an appeal got on the docket, the same amount of time would have passed as it would if Maeve went about completing her community service.

"What's got you so rankled, Counselor? Doesn't seem like such a bad houseguest to me. Even if she was, that new place of yours looks big enough that you wouldn't have to bump into each other if you didn't want to. If you did, well, that would be another matter entirely."

Whether he intended to or not, Mac had hit the so-called nail on the head. There'd be no *bumping* going on as long as I was Maeve's attorney, and as long as that writ bond stayed in effect, I was exactly that.

Another call came in, and when I checked the screen, I saw it was Money. "I'll get back to you, Mac."

I heard him chuckling when I hung up. Glad he thought it was funny.

"Hammer," I answered.

"I just got a call from Maeve."

I rubbed the top of my head with my left hand. "Yeah?"

"She asked me to come to Texas and see—"

"Stop right there. As I told you before, your presence here will do more harm than good. Speaking of good, it won't hurt your princess of a sister one bit to suffer a few consequences of her actions. The judge was right when he said she has a blatant disrespect for the law. If she wants to reside in the United States, it's high time she learned that she is not above following the same rules the rest of us have to. I don't care how much money she has."

My back was to the door, but I spun around when it slammed. *Great.* She'd heard every word I said.

"Money, I'll call you back." I raced down the stairs, where I heard another door slam. By the time I followed her outside, Maeve was halfway across the meadow and headed toward the fenced-off area where we kept the bulls. I broke into a run, knowing damn well if she got to it and didn't see any of them, she'd probably jump the fence, having no idea what she was getting herself into.

"Maeve, stop!" I shouted.

"Sod off and leave me alone!" she shouted back.

"Fuck," I groaned when she was over that fence before I could stop her. I only hoped there were no bulls in the vicinity. When I heard her scream, my hope was quashed.

I jumped the fence with an ease that shocked me and saw her and one of our biggest bulls facing off.

"Whatever you do, don't turn around and don't run." God, I hoped this wasn't one of the times I should've used reverse psychology. "Back away slowly. Keep your eyes on him."

She took two steps backwards and did the exact thing I told her not to. When she started to run, so did the bull. As she raced toward me, I went around her to get between her and the charging animal.

Much like I'd seen the bullfighters do at rodeos, I waved my hands, yelled, and jumped up and down. Within seconds, the bull's attention was on me. Unfortunately, it was too late to back away and have him lose interest. He charged me full bore. I side-stepped the beast and ran in the opposite direction, zigzagging to throw off the animal's momentum. I reached the fence and dove over it seconds before the bull caught up with me.

I rolled onto my back, shielding my eyes from the sun. When I landed on the ground, I rested and tried to catch my breath.

"Hammer?" I could feel Maeve crouch down next to me. "Are you okay?"

"I will be. Damn, I'm out of shape."

"I'm sorry."

I moved my arm from across my eyes, propped myself up on my elbows, and looked at her. "So am I."

"I'd rather not—"

"Look at me," I said, grabbing her arm when she went to stand. "I'm sorry for what you overheard.

I was angry, but not at you. I shouldn't have said those things."

"Why not? It's what you believe, isn't it?"

"Not entirely."

She laughed, but not because she thought it was funny. The angry look on her face intensified. "Which part don't you believe? The part where I'm a princess or that I have a blatant disrespect for the laws of the country I am so privileged to be permitted to reside in. I am a US citizen, and I pay taxes, Hammer. A great amount of them, actually."

I let go of her arm, but rather than getting up, Maeve sat on her bottom.

"I'm sorry, okay?" she repeated, looking everywhere but at me. "I'm obviously less pleased about this than you are, but I don't know what's to be done about it."

"Maeve?" She turned her head more, so I was looking at the back of it. "Dublin?"

"What?" she snapped.

"I'm not angry with you. I'm not even angry with the judge. If you want to know the truth, I wasn't ready for you to leave."

She spun around. *"Did you ask him to do this?"*

I laughed at the look of horror on her face. "No. I didn't. But the idea that we'd both be returning to our normal lives already, well... I knew I'd miss you."

She scoffed.

"It's true. It isn't every day a man gets to have such a beautiful woman sleeping in his bed, even if he isn't sleeping there with her."

"Hammer, I...I'm not..."

"Look, don't think I'm trying to pull the same thing Bobby did. For one, I'm too old for you. Two, I'm your attorney. Three, if I were going to try to seduce you, this wouldn't be how I'd go about it."

She studied me. "How *would* you go about it?"

I stared at her a long time before I responded. "I'm your attorney," I repeated.

"If you weren't?" Her voice was breathy, her tone deeper.

"That would be an entirely different story."

"You said we needed to talk."

"Yeah, we do. Let's go back to the house." It took a bit of effort, but I was able to stand. Tomorrow, though, I'd be sore as hell.

On our return, I thought through exactly what I wanted to say to Maeve. Should I tell her what I'd overheard when she was behind the closed doors of my bedroom and that it was the reason I'd left earlier? She'd probably be mortified, and that was my reason for not being honest earlier.

We'd just gotten to the house when my cell phone rang. I motioned to the Adirondack chairs and took a seat when she did.

"Hey, Mac. What's up?"

"Sorry to be calling again, but this is important."

I almost groaned. What now? "Go on."

"When we left your place earlier, I realized how serious my brother's drinking has gotten. That he drove drunk was a wake-up call for both of us. I decided it's time I stepped in."

"I'm sorry, Mac," I added.

"Appreciate it, Hammer. Listen, there's something I want to run by Maeve and you."

"She's right here. I can put the phone on speaker unless you want to talk with her privately." Although, as her attorney, I really shouldn't have made that offer.

"Speaker's good, Counselor." Mac obviously thought the same thing I had.

"Go ahead."

"Hey, Dublin." Maeve smiled, and so did I.

"Hey, Mac," she responded.

"As I just told Hammer, my brother's behavior of late has made me realize he needs more help than I can give him."

"If you're thinking rehab, it's the best thing for him," I said.

"Yeah, something like that. Anyway, it means, without him at the helm at the Long Branch, my inclination is to close the place down for a while at least."

"No!" Maeve gasped. "I mean, sorry, but that will be very detrimental to it as a business."

"I agree, and that's the reason for my call. Maeve, if you're still interested in buying the place, I have a proposal for you."

"Go ahead," I said when she nodded.

"It'll take some time for you to make arrangements to get the liquor license. Hammer, this is where you come in. Until her various charges get dismissed, the liquor board isn't going to look at the application too favorably."

"I agree."

"My proposal is this. The *two* of you go under contract on the Branch. Once Maeve has completed the terms of her sentencing, she should be able to get a license on her own. After that, it's a simple ownership transfer."

Maeve's eyes opened wide.

"You've given this a lot of thought," I said.

"The last thing my brother needs now is an assault charge. I've got a bargain to uphold."

I wanted to tell him neither Maeve nor I would hold him to it, but it wasn't my place to without conferring with her first.

"How does going under contract keep it open?" she asked.

"If you're interested in moving forward with the sale, we can structure the purchase so it doesn't finalize until the liquor board approves the license. In the meantime, you manage it."

"Can you give us some time to talk this over?" I asked.

"Of course. But the clock is ticking, Hammer. I'm sure as hell not opening the place up tonight myself."

"Got it." I ended the call. There was a lot more to this than Maeve agreeing to Mac's proposal. I had to as well.

"Taking myself out of the equation, my first question before we discuss some of the other things Mac presented is do *you* still want to buy the Long Branch?"

"I do."

"Why?"

"I can't answer that."

"I gotta ask. Do you have any idea what goes into running a place that size?"

"You're assuming I've no experience, is that it?"

"If you did, you wouldn't want a place like the Branch."

"I suppose you haven't heard of Mary Donoghue's, then."

"Of course I have." It was one of the most well-known pubs in Ireland, although it was far more than that. It was said a few of the world's most successful bands got their start at their location in Dublin. I'd also heard they'd expanded throughout the UK. "Did you work at one of them?"

Maeve laughed. "My mother was Mary as was her mother before her and her mother before that, reaching as far back as ten generations."

"Are you saying your mother was Mary Donoghue?"

"Aye."

"If they were all named Mary, how come your name is Maeve?"

She shook her head. "As with each of them, Maeve is my middle name."

"Then, you know it isn't an easy business."

"What about you? You're part of this, at least initially. Have you ever worked in a bar?"

I nodded. "All through college."

"I *know* the business, Hammer. Better than most. The Long Branch is already successful. I can make it more so."

"You also know your brother isn't in favor of you doing this. With good reason."

"Does that mean you're saying no?"

"If I were saying no, that's what I would've said."

"I'm aware of my brother's opinion; what's yours?"

"You're going to have to assemble a crew you trust. Since you intended to buy it on your own, do you have people in mind?"

"I've gotten to know key personnel quite well. I wouldn't disrupt the staff, particularly with Bobby going…away." She leaned forward and wrapped her arms around her bent legs. "What about you, Hammer? You said to take you out of the equation, but Mac's proposal hinges on you."

12

Maeve

I held my breath, waiting what felt like hours for him to answer. Would he refuse, citing the same reasons my brother had? Kellen's primary concern was that the place had once been a known hangout for the Aryan Brotherhood of Texas. While I understood that being a factor, I had my own reasons for wanting to proceed—ones I hadn't shared with him and didn't intend to.

It was the only way I could be there often enough that if the bloody bastard who'd stole one of my family's most valuable possessions came into the place the private detectives said he frequented, he'd find me waiting.

I'd spent as much time there over the last several months as I could, even trying to get a job, not that Bobby would hire me. The *feckin' eejit* had no idea I was part of one of the most successful pub-owning families in all of Europe. Even my brother—half brother—had no real idea of where the Donoghue wealth came from.

My grandmum used to say it was the cobbler's bairns who had no shoes. In this case, it was my brother, who was the director of one of the most powerful intelligence agencies in the world, who'd not bothered to look into the family his father married into. Granted, he was a child then and living in America, attending boarding school. And, in terms of his position now, our family was certainly not in the business of anything illegal.

I looked over at Hammer, who was studying me.

"Do you know why he's against it?" he asked.

"Probably the same reason you are. You both think I don't have what it takes to run it."

He shook his head. "I didn't say I was against it."

"I can glean you're hesitant."

"There's more to the Branch's story than you may know. Two years ago, there were a series of incidents in the bar, involving the Aryan Brotherhood of Texas. Bobby worked hard to keep them out of the place before and after. With Mac's help, of course."

"I'm aware it used to be an ABT hangout. Are you implying, once I take over, I wouldn't be able to do as Bobby did?"

"They're rough customers, so to speak. If they hear there's a new owner without the same ties to law enforcement as the previous one, they're likely to try to overrun the place again."

"I see. So as I said, neither you nor Kellen believes I have what it takes to prevent that from happening."

He pulled a cigar out of his pocket and stuck it in his mouth.

"Are you going to light that?"

He shook his head.

"Why, then?"

He took the cigar out of his mouth. "Nervous habit."

"This conversation is making you nervous?"

"I'm just saying the ABT may be rougher than you're used to."

I laughed. "You obviously haven't spent much time in Dublin."

"Not the same."

I took a deep breath in order to keep my temper in check. Losing it would do me no good. "There are more than one hundred and twenty-five gangs active in the city. They are responsible for ten times that many deaths each year, both rival gang members and innocent victims caught in the crossfire. If you think Mary

Donoghue's was immune to them, you're dead wrong. We've battled decade upon decade to keep them out of our pubs, to resist their extortion tactics. The Aryan Brotherhood may be made up of 'rough characters,' but none worse than the Kinahans or the Byrnes. I could name dozens more."

"You feel like taking a ride?"

I scrunched my eyes. "What?"

"You know, in the car?"

The man had a habit of abruptly ending conversations in the most unusual ways. "Sure. Okay."

"There are some people I want you to meet. Good friends of mine."

"People you believe will talk me out of wanting to buy the Branch?"

Hammer laughed. "Maybe people who can help us."

"Us?"

"Come on, Dublin. Let's go."

"I'd like to change first."

He looked down at his dirt-covered trousers. "I should do the same."

We went inside and up the stairs, realizing at the same time that we were both headed to the master bedroom.

"Go ahead," I said, motioning to the door.

"No, you can go first."

"I'll likely take longer."

"Right. I'll just grab some clothes and get out of your way."

He came out of the closet moments later, with garments tossed over his arm but without a shirt. "Laundry's in there," he offered by way of explanation, I supposed.

"Wait," I said when he walked past. "Is that Dylan Thomas?" The words inked into his skin were taken from one of my favorite poems. "Do not go gentle into that good night. Rage, rage against the dying of the light."

While Thomas saw it as fighting death, I saw it as never giving up the fight to be the kind of woman my mum would admire. Part of that would be getting back the thing that was taken from me—the thing that belonged to her and her mother before that. I would continue to fight on behalf of generations of Donoghue women in the same way they would have if what was done to me had been done to them.

I stood close enough to Hammer that I could feel his labored breathing. If I wanted to, I could reach out and run my fingers over the words—and damn, did I want to.

I raised my hand slowly to see if he'd stop me. Instead, he closed his eyes and raised his face to the ceiling. Even then, I could see his furrowed brow. It was as though he was steeling himself for the pain he knew was coming. I traced my favorite word in the poem—rage—with the nail of my index finger. Hammer lowered his head and opened his eyes but didn't speak. I placed my palm on his chest and could feel his heart beating beneath it.

"Dublin," he growled.

"Find me another lawyer."

Those words appeared to snap him out of the trance we'd both been under, and he took a step back. "Even if I did, which I can't…"

"Why not?" I whispered, closing the distance he'd put between us.

"Dammit," he groaned at the same time he grabbed the back of my neck and brought his mouth to mine.

I whimpered at the sheer power behind his kiss, the way his mouth dominated mine, and the feel of his hardness when he grabbed my arse and brought my pelvis in line with his.

He abruptly broke the kiss and rested his forehead against mine. "We…can't…do…this."

I twisted out of his grasp. I'd already made it clear I wanted to. I wouldn't bloody beg. Before I could stalk out of the room, his arm snaked around my waist, and he pulled my body against his.

"You have no idea how much I've wanted to touch you, kiss you, feel your amazing body plastered up against mine. *No fucking idea*."

"You're wrong. I have every fucking idea." I ground my arse against the bulge in his trousers.

His mouth was next to my ear. "Not yet."

"I don't like waiting."

He chuckled. "Maybe it'll be good for you."

I tried to wriggle out of his arms, but he held tighter.

"I was joking." His chest expanded with the deep breath he inhaled. "God, you smell good."

"Hammer."

"And I sure do like hearing my name on your lips."

Had he heard me the other day? Is that why he'd left in such a hurry? I couldn't ask. I was already too embarrassed. This time when I wriggled, he let me go. "We should get ready if we're leaving."

"You're right." The moment over, he left the room.

"Where are we going?" I asked once we were in the Porsche.

"King-Alexander Ranch. Ever heard of it?"

"Of course I have. It isn't far from the Long Branch."

"Most of the hands hang out there, some of the guys I work with too."

"Other lawyers?"

He shook his head and half laughed. "Nah. I'm the only one of those in the group. You may recognize some of my friends, though."

Apart from keeping watch for one man in particular, I hadn't paid much attention to the other bar patrons. When I was there, my purpose was very single-minded. If I were working there and when I eventually owned it, that would change. Perhaps meeting these friends of Hammer's would be a step in that direction. However, I doubted very much they'd become my friends too.

Other than people like Billy and Alicia, who weren't really friends, more people I knew because I was a regular at their restaurant, there weren't many people in my life who rose above acquaintance status. I kept my distance intentionally.

In Dublin, I was well recognized. Here, no one knew a thing about me, and I liked it that way. How many times had a mate's attitude changed once they found out I was connected to Donoghue's? It was as though a switch went on, and I went from someone they wanted to know to someone who could do something for them. I fucking hated it.

Hammer didn't seem like that, though. He did more for me than I did for him. "Who's paying you?" I asked when it suddenly dawned on me I should be making arrangements to do that.

"I'm on retainer," he responded without looking at me.

"For whom? My brother?"

"No. People connected to him."

"People I don't know are paying you to represent me?"

"Not exactly, but yeah."

"No. Absolutely not. I pay my own way."

"It isn't a big deal, Dublin."

"It is to me, *Drip*. Jesus."

"We'll talk about it later," he said as he drove up to the ranch's gate.

"C'mon in, Hammer," a voice said through a speaker I couldn't see from where I sat. The man speaking sounded vaguely familiar. Probably because his accent was similar to the man next to me in the car.

"Ready?" he asked when we pulled up to a large ranch house.

"Hello!" a man who came out onto the porch once we'd gotten out of the car shouted. A woman followed him and waved.

"Welcome to King-Alexander," she said when we approached. "I'm Darrow Alexander."

"Maeve McTiernan." I shook her hand. "You're English?"

The woman laughed. "That, I am. However, my husband insists I sound more and more like a Texan each day."

She didn't to me at all.

The man I assumed was her husband stepped forward. "Hi, I'm Quint."

I repeated my name and shook his hand.

"Shall we go inside?" Darrow asked. "Edge and Rebel should be here shortly."

Edge and Rebel? What kind of names were those? Sounded to me like gang members.

"Can I get you anything to drink? A pint, perhaps?"

"I'll take a beer, please," Hammer answered when I looked at him.

"Me too, thanks."

"It's a little too chilly to be outside. Hope you don't mind if we stay in here." She pointed to a large round dining table. It reminded me of the family tables we had at Donoghue's.

"This is lovely," I said when she put a basket of crisps on the table along with charcuterie and a baguette.

Darrow sat beside me, and I looked around but had no idea where Hammer had gone off to. "How long have you been in America?" she asked, handing me a plate and napkin.

"Not quite a year. You?"

"Off and on for a few years but more permanently since Quint and I married."

"Are you from Bedfordshire?" I asked.

Darrow blushed. "I forget that people from the UK don't lump us all into the same accent. And yes, I am. Dublin?"

"The very place."

"So, what brought you here?" While the woman was merely trying to be polite, she had no idea what a landmine her question was.

"I visited and didn't want to leave." I anticipated her next question and answered before she asked. "My father was from the US, so I hold dual citizenship."

"That's bloody nice, isn't it? It's not a problem now, since Quint and I are married, but prior, the paperwork made me a wreck. Not a fan. Of paperwork, that is."

"Aye," I murmured, wondering again where Hammer was.

"Hello?" I heard another woman's distinctively American-sounding voice call out.

"We're in here," Darrow answered.

"Hi, I'm Rebel. Lucy, but no one ever calls me that." She held out her hand, and I shook it.

"I'm Maeve."

Rebel pulled a chair out, removed her jacket, and sat down.

"Where's Edge?" Darrow asked.

"Quint and Hammer intercepted him on our way in." Rebel rolled her eyes. "When you're dating, they never leave your side. Once you're married, it's like there's a rule that we have to separate by gender whenever we get together with friends." She leaned forward and rested her arms on the table. "I hear you're buying the Branch."

"Oh, right. I heard that too," said Darrow.

"It's not official yet."

Rebel looked over her shoulder and leaned farther forward. "I heard Bobby is headed to rehab. Someone else said he's ill."

"Rebel, those are rumors." Darrow turned to me. "Either way, how would it affect the sale?"

"I'm not certain yet." I wasn't used to sharing my business with anyone, let alone two women I'd met only a few minutes ago.

"Well, if you need any help, I could lend a hand," Rebel offered.

"Doing what?"

Both women laughed.

"Sorry, that came out in a way I didn't intend it to."

"It's okay. I like your bluntness. I can wait tables, or if you need someone in the kitchen, I can fill in there too."

"Rebel is a chef," Darrow explained.

"Oh, how lovely."

"But I've also waitressed and been behind the bar."

"There?"

"Yeah. Before…you know. Actually, maybe you don't know."

I looked between the two women.

"There was some unpleasantness with an unsavory element not too long ago."

Rebel laughed. "Darrow's left the building, and the duchess has returned in her place."

Darrow smacked her.

"Duchess?"

"I'm not. Although my brother is a duke."

"Of Bedfordshire?"

"Yes."

I recognized the look on Darrow's face. It was similar to mine when I encountered someone who knew more about me than I would've liked. "Sorry. Not my business."

"No matter," she said, patting my hand. "It's hardly a secret."

I turned to Rebel. "Was the 'unsavory element' the ABT?"

"Yes." Same look from her.

"I'm sorry," I repeated.

"Don't be. Like with Darrow, it isn't a secret. Just a time of my life I'd rather not think about."

"It brought you and Edge together."

"You're right, Dar. He's my silver lining."

"And you're mine, sweetness." A man who also had an English accent leaned down and kissed Rebel's cheek. "Hi," he said, turning to me. "I'm Keon Edgemon."

Hammer pulled out the chair beside me and sat down, turning it to face me when all three men gathered around the table. "How's it going?" he asked.

"Good. Fine."

"I thought you might like Darrow and Rebel."

That type of comment would've bothered me spoken by anyone else, but from Hammer, it didn't. Or maybe it was because I *did* like them.

"Mac called."

I looked at him. "Yeah?"

"He's going to shut the Branch down for a couple of days."

"I see." I wasn't happy about that decision, but Hammer and I still hadn't come to an agreement about going under contract on the bar. Maybe he had no interest in doing so.

"Wait. He's going to shut down *the Branch*?" asked Rebel. She pushed her chair back and stood. "That's a *terrible* idea."

Hammer turned to me. "There's a solution."

"Is there?" I asked.

"Well, I don't know about y'all, but I'm not gonna let him do that if I can help it." Rebel looked at her husband.

"I've been known to pour a pint or two," he said. "I'm sure Quint has too."

The other man nodded. "What about you, Hammer?"

"I'm in."

"I'm fairly useless in the kitchen, but I'm willing to help if someone tells me what to do," offered Darrow.

"What do you think, Dublin? Are you in?" Hammer asked me.

"Bobby does have a full staff, but since he won't be there tonight, I'm sure he'd appreciate the extra help."

"You're buyin' the place, so you must have some bar experience," said Rebel.

I took a deep breath and let it out slowly. Was I really about to do this? "My family owned Mary Donoghue's," I blurted before I could talk myself out of it.

"Are you serious?" asked Edge.

"*Gawd*, I love Mary's," added Darrow, calling it the same thing most regulars did.

"What's that?" Rebel asked.

"Only the best pub in all of Ireland. Well, now England too." Edge leveled a gaze at Darrow. "But don't go telling anyone I said that."

She motioned with her hand like she was zipping her lips.

"Should I call him back?" Hammer asked me.

I shrugged. "Why not?"

"Does the family still run Mary's?" Edge asked when Hammer walked away to ring Mac.

"I'm really all that's left." Hard to fathom the lineage of Mary Donoghue would end with me, unless I one day had a daughter of my own. I'd never considered it a possibility. I still didn't.

There were times I felt guilty for leaving Ireland, but the truth was, the reason my net worth had increased so significantly from my original inheritance was that I'd taken the parent organization public the year after my father passed. While I owned the majority of the stock, that Mary's was no longer "family run," gave me freedom I'd never experienced before. It made me realize I wanted a fresh start—somewhere new and different.

"We have crews running each location for years," I explained when I realized Edge was still waiting for an answer.

"Nice you can trust the lot of them," he commented.

The ones who had been around for years, yes. I'd learned a painful and expensive lesson when I attempted to bring in someone new. It was one reason I wanted to hang on to as many of Bobby's employees as possible. They had a stake in the place, and regulars would appreciate they'd stuck around. It was an endorsement of sorts for the new ownership.

Hammer's friends helping was a brilliant move on his part, especially Rebel, who'd worked there before. The others too, who were regulars themselves.

"Mac will meet us there," Hammer said when he returned to the kitchen, where everyone waited.

"You're sure about this?" I collectively asked.

Rebel put her arm through mine. "Just try to keep us away."

13

Hammer

Exactly what I'd hoped would happen had. My friends had volunteered to help Maeve, and she jumped into taking charge with both feet. Of that, I'd expected nothing less.

The place was packed, as was typical, although more than usual on a Tuesday. It also seemed like the energy had changed. There was an excitement in the air I hadn't felt before. News traveled fast in this part of the world, or maybe it was in every part of the world. I wouldn't be surprised if people had heard Bobby was selling or that he'd gone away for a while and the new owner would be here, so that's why they were too.

Whether that was the case or not, Maeve was a marvel. Anyone who wondered if she had enough experience to handle a place like the Branch would be proven wrong, watching her tonight.

Whether the ABT raised their ugly heads was yet to be seen. While Maeve believed she could handle them, she wouldn't be facing them alone. It was why

I'd asked Quint if we could step outside to chat earlier and why I'd intercepted Edge on his way in.

I gave them a rundown of what had happened over the course of the last few days—including Bobby going to rehab or wherever Mac intended to get him the help he needed—along with the sheriff's offer to Maeve and me.

"I'm going to ask Deck for backup with this," I told the two men.

"Good call, getting the team involved," said Edge. While the Invincibles partners, like he was, were all equal, Decker Ashford was the unofficial point person on the majority of missions in the United States. Edge's older brother, Lennox, also known as Lynx, was in charge of East Coast ops. Cortez "Rile" DeLéon, the man who'd founded the firm, oversaw Europe.

Quint nodded. While he didn't work for the covert operation in any capacity, as the son of MI6's current chief, husband of a current MI6 agent, as well as Deck's best friend from childhood, he was almost as much of an insider as I was. Actually, maybe more so.

"There's unfinished business between us and the ABT. You know that," Edge reminded me, but he was right—I hadn't forgotten.

"What can I do?" I asked Maeve, who appeared lost in thought.

"Sorry. What did you say?"

"I asked if I could help."

She looked around the busy bar and restaurant. Everything appeared to be running smoothly, but I didn't have the same level of experience she did.

"Ask me to dance."

"Really?"

She nodded. "It was an unspoken rule at Mary Donoghue's. If you didn't make it a point to dance at least once a night, you didn't belong there."

"Even when it was busy?"

"Especially when it was."

By the time we got to the dance floor, a song had come on that was slow enough for a nightclub two-step. It was a little different than a regular two-step and perfect when a man wanted to hold a woman in his arms as they danced.

"You're a good dancer," Maeve said after a couple of minutes.

"Thank you, ma'am. You are too." It didn't surprise me any, especially after watching her do yoga. I tightened my grip around her waist and showed off a little, spinning us both until she giggled.

"I like this rule," I said when the song ended but she didn't make a move to leave the floor.

"You'd be surprised what it does for morale. Not to mention, the customers love it."

"What other things did you do at Mary Donoghue's that you'd want to implement here?"

She shrugged. "I have a few ideas."

"Tell me."

"Maybe later. Now I want to dance."

I was more than happy to oblige, especially when she pressed her body against mine. This time when the song ended, Maeve stood on her tiptoes and kissed my cheek. "You need to find me a different lawyer, Drip."

She twisted out of my arms and went behind the bar, motioning to Rebel to take a break. I expected her and Edge to wind up dancing like Maeve and I had when she made a beeline in his direction. Instead, I saw the two of them head-to-head, looking toward the door I couldn't see from where I stood.

Edge gave me a head nod, and I joined them. As I walked past the bar, I knew by the look on Maeve's face that she'd seen the same thing they had. My guess was word got out to the ABT already about Bobby being gone and they were back to mark their territory. Not on my fuckin' watch, they wouldn't be.

"Where's Steel?" I asked Edge as soon as I was close enough that he could hear me.

"Working at a place in Austin."

"We need to get him back here."

"Roger that."

"Who's bouncing tonight?"

"Tres, Rojo, and Bunker," Rebel answered. "There's a couple of other guys I don't know on tonight."

"Get 'em vetted." I motioned to the one I recognized as Bunker.

"Give Edge the names of the new guys. *Now!*" I added when he started to walk away but with his hand on his earpiece.

"Sure thing, boss."

Edge pulled out his cell and tapped his screen, entering the names Bunker gave him, I assumed. While he did that, I called Mac.

"We need help."

"I heard. I've got a crew on the way. I'll be right behind 'em."

"Who told you?"

"Tres called the minute the fuckers walked in the door. They're banned for life, and they know it."

I was glad to hear Tres had taken the initiative to call Mac. Later, I'd mention to Maeve that she might want to make him head bouncer.

"Deck's on it," Edge said after I ended my call.

"Good. Who else is around?"

"Ink, and before you say anything, I already messaged him. He and Rip are on their way. Rip is bringing some of the hands."

"Good. We'll shut these assholes down so fast they'll know better than to try this shit again. As Mac said, they know they're banned." I looked over my shoulder and made eye contact with Maeve, who was walking our way. Instead, I headed her off.

"It's handled," I said, taking her hand and leading her toward the back room and the office.

"What do you mean 'it's *handled*'?" God, her Irish temper lit me on fire.

"What I mean is, you've got a team of bouncers who know exactly who just walked in the front door. Tres called Mac the second they did. Rip will arrive shortly with some of the other guys we work with."

"The cavalry is on the way, then?"

I smiled. "I guess you could call it that."

She took a deep breath and let it out slowly. I could visibly see her relent. "I didn't think they'd descend this quickly."

"I'm surprised too, although I shouldn't be, not with as fast as word of Bobby needing to leave town spread to King-Alexander."

She rested her butt on a table and rolled her shoulders. "I don't know him well, but I get the impression he's never done anything like this."

"He hasn't." I hadn't said a word to anyone about the blood I saw on the handkerchief and wouldn't now. Either his drinking had gotten that bad or something more serious was wrong. I had a feeling it was the latter.

"Sad." Maeve looked into my eyes and held out her hand. "I could use a *cwtch*."

"A *what*?"

"A cuddle. You know, a hug?"

I took her hand, pulled her to her feet, and as much as I knew I shouldn't, drew her body close.

Like she did after our dance, after a few seconds had passed, she pulled back and kissed my cheek. Before she could say it, I did. "I know. I need to find you a new attorney." I had to admit, the idea was growing on me. First, however, I had to figure out what to tell her brother.

By the time Maeve and I returned to the bar area, there was no sign of anyone from the ABT. "What happened?" I asked Edge.

"He showed up and brought Rage with him."

I followed his line of sight, but I already knew who he was talking about. Breckin "Ink" Ryan was the biggest, bulkiest bodybuilder I'd ever seen, and that included the guy who won the Mr. Olympia title eight consecutive years.

At close to six feet, the guy had to weigh in at over three hundred pounds, and every ounce of it was solid muscle.

Garrett "Rage" Williams, the man Edge said Ink brought with him, must've been training with Ink because he looked twice as big as the last time I saw him. I hoped the Invincibles didn't need either of them for a mission anytime soon.

The rest of the night flew by, and before I knew it, Maeve was announcing last call by ringing the same cowbell Bobby always had.

I couldn't remember a time I'd been as tired as I was tonight, yet part of me was as exhilarated as I'd been after completing a successful mission back in my Marine Raider days.

I stayed out of the way while the bartenders and servers closed out their tabs and tips and got the place ready for the cleaning crew Maeve said would arrive at five after two.

"Damn, I don't know what Bobby's been bringing in lately, but tonight was a helluva lot better than when I used to work here," said Rebel, counting the money in the bar's tip jar.

"It was a much better night than his recent averages," added Maeve, closing out the register and credit card machines. "If people came because they're curious, I'll gladly keep things interesting and welcome them back. Everyone but the ABT, that is. Those bloody bastards."

I looked over at Rebel, knowing what she was thinking before she started to say it. "It's my fault—"

"No, it isn't. This is about territory and nothing more."

"He's right," said Edge, walking up and putting his arm around his wife. Over their heads, my eyes met Maeve's as they had several other times tonight.

"What do you think?" I asked, joining her behind the bar.

"It was a great first night, if you can call it that. I mean, Bobby does still own the place. Maybe once he's back, he'll change his mind about selling."

"Maybe, except Mac will do everything in his power to make sure he delivers on his promise."

"Aye," she said under her breath. "I'm beat. Been a while since I've done this."

"Longer for me, Dublin. I'm definitely feeling my age."

"The next three nights will be harder."

I put my arm around her shoulders. "Then, I say we call this one a night and get some sleep."

"My truck is still in the lot."

I doubted Judge Ringer or even Mac expected I'd have my eyes on Maeve every minute. It was more that I was responsible for making sure she didn't jump bail.

However, it was late, and she'd already admitted she was beat. "I can have Rip bring it to the ranch, if that's okay with you."

"He wouldn't mind?"

"Wouldn't matter if he did," I said, winking. "Although I doubt he would."

"Please, then. I'd appreciate it."

"Keys?"

"Under the left rear bumper."

I raised a brow, and she laughed.

"If you saw it, you'd know no one would want to steal it."

I sent Rip a text, and he gave me a thumbs-up from across the room. "Come on. Let's get outta here."

"I need to lock up."

"I can do it for you," Tres offered.

"You're sure?"

"Did it for Bobby every night."

"I'll take you up on it, then. Thank you."

"He's a good guy," I told her once we were in the car. "He called Mac as soon as he saw the ABT fuckers walk in."

Maeve cringed. "I wish he wouldn't have bothered him with this."

"I'll tell you what; the man lives for his job, and I mean that literally. I'm sure you saw him when he came in."

"You're right. He did look happier than when we saw him earlier."

"So, don't fault Tres. I think he did the right thing."

She covered her mouth when she yawned and rested her head against the seat.

"Let's get you home and into bed."

She opened one eye and looked at me. "If only."

14

Maeve

While Hammer smiled, I knew he was just as affected by me as I was him, especially after the kiss we'd shared earlier in the day. God, the man was good at that. It was all I could do not to reach over and cup the bulge between his legs and tell him everything I'd do once I got him naked.

I would, too, if it weren't for the fact that his being my lawyer seemed to be a line he wouldn't cross. I respected him for it.

When I was sure he was focused on the road, I opened my eyes and studied him. He'd said he was feeling his age, and yet of all the hot cowboys in the bar tonight, none did it for me the way he did. The way the muscles of his arms strained against the fabric of his shirt in the same way those of his legs did against his tight jeans. I thought about how he'd looked shirtless and couldn't stop myself from groaning.

Shocking me, Hammer reached over, covered my hand with his, and squeezed but didn't say anything.

"You're aware you're hot as fuck, aren't you?"

Hammer smiled. "You're good for my ego, Dublin, and right back at you."

"Believe me, it isn't your ego I want to stroke, Drip."

Rather than smile, the look he gave me was as heated as the area between my legs. He shook his head and looked away. "Your brother would never forgive me," he muttered without facing me.

"Kellen is hardly my keeper."

"You're right. He trusted me to be, and that isn't something I take lightly."

"You would have to be the honorable sort, wouldn't you?"

"If you could read my mind, you'd know I'm not."

"Read it for me. Tell me what you're thinking."

Hammer gave a hearty laugh. "You better watch it, Dublin, or the next time your brother threatens to come to Texas, I'll let him."

"You won't. I know better."

"You're right. My only goal is to get you cleared of the remaining charges so you can move on with the rest of your life. Money coming here would not expedite the process."

"What happens once I can move on?"

"I can't answer that except to say I'll no longer be your attorney. I wonder if you'll still be as eager once it's no longer forbidden."

I groaned, but this time in irritation. "Now you sound just like Kellen. Congratulations, you have succeeded in completely ruining the mood."

By the time he pulled through the gates of his ranch, I could barely keep my eyes open. I'd grown up working at Mary's, putting in hours longer than the ones I had today. Even though it had been several weeks since I last had, I felt soft, and I didn't like it.

I scowled at Hammer when he asked if he could get me anything before I went upstairs. "If I want anything, I'm more than capable of getting it for myself." Rather than risk being ruder, I stalked up the staircase and threw myself on the bed. While my brain knew I should undress, clean my teeth, and get under the duvet, my body was unwilling to cooperate.

When I woke sometime near dawn, it took me a minute to get my bearings and figure out where I was. Hammer's house—and he was asleep in another room.

Argh. That man made me crazy. Why couldn't I have less complicated taste in men? Or why couldn't the men I was attracted to be simpler? I'd always gone for the bad boys, until the one who was so bad, he'd gotten away with taking something precious from me.

Cormac Moran was the bastard's name, and I'd been the one to hire him as general manager of Mary's in Dublin. It was the worst mistake I'd made in my life. Not only was he a master womanizer, he also excelled in theft. *Grand theft.* He'd pay, though. I'd see to it. Not that he or anyone else knew the true value of the "trinket" he'd pilfered. Probably just thought it was something pretty he could gift to the next woman he scammed.

The next two nights were a repeat of the first except busier and without the drama of the ABT showing up. Something told me they had no intention of staying away permanently.

The third night—Friday—was an entirely different story. Not only did more of the ABT show up, but after they'd been escorted out for a second time, another man showed up. Someone I recognized from Mary's.

He was a friend of Cormac's, who, like him, was American—from Austin, in fact. The bastard thief had wanted to hire him, but by that point, I was already questioning my decision to bring Cormac on. So I didn't approve it. It was the first knockdown argument he and I had. They only got worse from there.

I took another look at the man. While I wasn't certain he'd recognize me, there was a possibility, and I couldn't risk it. I racked my brain but couldn't recall his name. Maybe it was just the idea that all these weeks of waiting were about to pay off that left my head spinning.

"Everything okay?" Hammer asked.

"I've a bit of a headache, but I'm sure it'll pass."

"Have you taken anything for it?"

"Um. No."

"I'll get you something."

He came back a few minutes later with my choice of medication. "Why don't you take a break, maybe eat something?"

If I stayed in the office, I could monitor the security cameras in the event Cormac also arrived, but be out of the line of sight of his friend. "Good idea."

"What do you want to eat?"

"Um. A burger?"

Hammer studied me.

"What?"

"It must be a pretty bad headache."

"What makes you say that?"

"First, you're ghostly white, and second, I don't think I've ever heard you say 'um,' and you've just used it twice."

"I'm always pale, Hammer. I'm Irish." I attempted to joke.

"Not that pale." He got close enough that his mouth was near my ear. "You're lying to me, Dublin, and later, you're going to tell me why."

I escaped to the confines of the office and locked the door behind me. I needed to get my wits about me and quick.

A few minutes later, I heard the door handle jiggle, followed by a loud knock. *Feckin' hell.* I shouldn't have locked it before I got my dinner. I rushed over and threw the bolt. "Sorry. Habit."

Hammer came inside, carrying two burgers, both with fries. "Hope you don't mind if I join you."

"Of course not."

He was quiet while he ate—painfully slowly as usual. I, on the other hand, wolfed it down so quickly I felt nauseated.

He finally sat back in his chair and rubbed his belly. "Hope you're not still considering changing the menu."

I smirked. "You know I was joking."

"Yeah. So"—he picked up his knife and pointed at one of the security monitors where Cormac's friend was front and center—"wanna tell me who that guy is?"

"What do you mean?"

When Hammer raised a brow and scowled at me, it was reminiscent of my primary school days and being sent to the headmaster's office. *"No lying."*

"He looks like someone I recognize from Ireland, although I'm not certain it's him."

"Who is he, and what's he doing in Texas?"

"To be honest, I don't remember his name." That appeared to get him to settle down a little, probably because then I had told the truth.

"How did you know him?"

"Why? Are you jealous?"

He stood, moved his plate, and leaned over the desk. "Not even a little."

"Thanks a lot."

"*Because* you're lying again."

"He's a friend of someone I was once involved with, but it ended badly."

He sat down and folded his arms. "What was his name?"

"Why does it matter?"

"Because when you took one look at Mr. 'I Can't Remember His Name,' you turned white as a sheet."

"Have you ever considered you're not right about everything?"

"Some things I'm wrong about. Not this thing, however."

"He's not important." I was speaking about the friend, not Cormac, but at least Hammer wouldn't catch me in another lie.

"Is he the reason for your sudden headache?"

It dawned on me that if I hadn't been feeling guilty about lying, I never would've put up with his questioning me.

"Does this somehow relate to the bond you hold on me?"

"I don't hold it on you, and maybe."

"Well, I'm telling you it doesn't. Therefore, it's none of your business."

He pointed to the screen again. "Now, see? There's something going on with him too. Look at how he's casing the place while he's on his phone."

Hammer was right. It was almost as though he was looking for someone. *Feckin'* hell, was it me?

"I suppose I could always request a meeting with the judge, have the bond discharged, and you can figure your mess out on your own."

"I know you wouldn't do that."

"Or tell Mac the deal is off."

"You wouldn't do that either."

"Wanna try me?"

"Hammer, please let this go. It isn't worth these kinds of hysterics."

He threw his head back and laughed. "Hysterics? You're funny." When he leveled his gaze, his eyebrow was up again. "Look, you can start telling me the real story behind this guy, or you can find out just how *hysterical* I can get."

When I tried to get up to leave the office, he stood and put himself between me and the door.

"You're trapping me in here?"

"I guess I am because something about that guy affected you in such a way that I hardly recognize you. So until you decide to tell me the truth, I'm not backing off."

"You can sod off; that's what you can do."

15

Hammer

Maybe I wasn't taking the right approach. If I tried switching to nice cop, would she be more honest with me? Probably not. Still, I stepped aside to let her leave.

Instead, she turned around and sat down. "I'm quite independent."

"I'm aware."

"And I'm stubborn."

I nodded. "That too."

"You're *not* helping."

"I'm trying to help, but you won't let me."

"That's hardly the case. I've agreed to everything you've suggested."

I sat like she had, leaned forward, and rested my arms on the desk. "Something about that man made your entire demeanor change the minute he walked in." I looked up at the security screen, and so did Maeve. However, she didn't comment.

"Him being a friend of someone you were once in a relationship with, no matter how badly it ended, shouldn't cause such a reaction. Unless, of course, you killed the guy."

She glared at me.

"Well? Did you?"

"Of course I didn't," she responded through gritted teeth.

"Shot him, but didn't kill him?"

"You're not funny, Hammer. Not at all."

"I'm not trying to be. When you say it ended badly, give me the details."

"As I've already *said*, it isn't important."

"I disagree. It's so important you're continuing to lie about it."

"Hammer…"

"This guy." I pointed to the screen. "Are you afraid of him?"

She shook her head. "I'm not."

"What about the ex?"

"No."

There was something about the look on her face and the tone of her voice. "Should he be afraid of you?"

It took her a long time to answer, but when she did, I knew she was telling me the truth.

"He took something very precious to me."

If my brain were able to emit sound effects, it would be pinging. Dots were connecting like rapid-fire. That's why Maeve was in Texas, why she wanted to buy the Branch. He had some connection to it.

"What's his name?"

She hesitated. "I told you I don't recall."

"Not him," I motioned with my head. "The one who took something from you."

Her eyes were wide, and she shook her head.

"You don't trust me."

"It isn't that."

I rested against the back of the chair. "Of course it is. Just so you know, I get it. Four days ago, I got you out of jail. Before that, if I'd walked into a room, you wouldn't have noticed, let alone recognized me."

She smiled. "I would have noticed."

I smiled too. "Trust in a person takes time spent getting to know each other. We haven't had that. Still, if you ever need to, you can. Not just because I'm your lawyer."

"Thank you," she whispered.

"So, you hanging out in here for the rest of the night?"

Maeve took a deep breath and let it out slowly.

"Or just until he leaves?"

She nodded.

"I got ya covered." Before I walked out, I heard her ask me to wait.

"Yeah?"

"Thank you, Hammer," she repeated.

"You're welcome."

When I returned to the bar, I made eye contact with Edge and motioned him over.

"Yeah?"

"There's a guy at ten o'clock we need to keep our eye on."

"The one who's been texting since he came in? Hasn't ordered a drink?"

"He's the one."

"Do you think he's ABT?"

I shook my head. "He's someone from Maeve's past."

"Ah. Someone she doesn't want to know she's here."

"Exactly."

It wasn't that Edge and I had some kind of mental connection; it was more that noticing guys like the one we were talking about was what we were trained to do.

While I'd taken the law route rather than go to work directly for the CIA, my background wasn't that different from his. We'd both started out in the military and rose through the ranks to eventually be recruited into special ops. Me with the Marine Raiders and Force Recon. I didn't know the details of his career other than that before he signed on as a partner in the Invincibles, he'd been with MI5.

"I'll continue watching. You want me to alert the security guys?"

"Just Tres."

"Roger that."

After the first night, Edge had started wearing an earpiece with a mic just like the bouncers did. I knew the minute he'd told Tres to keep an eye on the guy.

I didn't like that Maeve felt she had to hide out, but I saw no alternative.

Thirty minutes later, the guy left. Tres followed, but returned almost right away.

"Tres saw him drive off," Edge walked over to tell me. "Bunker is on lot duty. He'll make sure to alert him if the guy returns."

"Were you able to get a clear shot of him?"

"Affirmative. Already sent it to Decker."

I motioned to his ear. "Get me a set before tomorrow night."

"Roger that," I heard him say when I walked away.

Maeve met me halfway between where I was and the office.

"The guys confirmed he's gone, but they'll be on the lookout if he returns."

She nodded but didn't seem any less jarred.

"Do you want me to take you back to the house?"

"I can't leave. Look at this place."

"I won't force you to do anything you don't want to do, but you *can* leave. There's a capable crew in place."

"I'd rather stay."

"How about a dance, then?"

I watched as she tried to talk herself either in or out of it. I couldn't tell which. Finally, she put her hand in mine. Just like the first night, the song playing was slow enough that I could hold her in my arms. Something I think we both needed.

If Decker was successful in identifying the man through facial recognition, I'd need to let Maeve know. Until then, he was gone and we could dance.

Maeve didn't say much the rest of the night, and on the ride home, she either fell asleep or feigned it.

We were about to get out of the car after I'd pulled into the garage when she put her hand on my arm. "I appreciate everything you're doing, Hammer. You and your friends, but you can't keep working at the bar every night."

"Sure, I can. I'm your partner for now, remember?"

"We haven't made that official."

"I got the impression Mac intended to let you work the place a few days to see if you still wanted to go through with the purchase. No one is going to hold you to doing so if you've changed your mind."

"I'd never."

"Why the sudden change? Before you seemed ambivalent."

Maeve got out of the car, so I did too.

"I'd forgotten how much I loved it."

"Me too, honestly."

"Mary's was great fun—most of the time, anyway."

The lawyer in me wanted to fire questions at her based on that statement, but we both needed sleep. I opened the door that led from the garage into the house. After the first night when she'd so adamantly informed me that if she wanted anything, she'd get it for herself, I hadn't made the offer again. Tonight, though, there was something I needed.

"Before we go upstairs…"

She raised a brow.

"Can I have a crutch?"

It took her a second before she smiled. "A *cwtch*?"

"Yeah. That."

When she stepped forward, I took her hand and led her upstairs. I might regret this in the morning, but tonight, I needed to hold Maeve in my arms. If she'd let me.

She didn't say a word as we walked side by side up to the second floor, nor when I led her into the master bedroom. "Just a *cwtch*," I murmured, walking over to the perfectly made bed. "Tell me if you don't want to do this."

"I want to, more than anything."

16

Maeve

I nearly wept with how good it felt just to be held. I couldn't remember how long it had been since I'd experienced anything beyond dancing. This was different in so many ways. No music. No other couples on a crowded dance floor. No steps to take. Just the sound of Hammer's heart beating beneath where my cheek rested. I loved how tightly he'd wrapped me in his arms, and prayed he wouldn't let go too soon. I closed my eyes and reveled in his comfort.

When I woke sometime later, I was still in the same position in Hammer's arms, but somehow, he'd covered us both with a blanket.

"Go back to sleep," he whispered when I raised my head. I had no intention of arguing. This felt far too good.

When I next opened my eyes, the sun was high in the sky, and I was on the bed alone. While that was somewhat disappointing, I hadn't felt this rested in months.

"Good morning," Hammer said, walking in moments later and carrying two cups of coffee.

"Bless you," I said when he handed one to me after I sat up and rested against the headboard. "What time is it?"

He looked at his watch. "In two minutes, it will be afternoon."

"Goodness. I slept later than normal."

"We both did." He sat down beside me on the bed, and I realized he was wearing different clothes than he had been when I fell asleep.

"How long have you been up?"

He raised his cup of coffee just slightly. "Long enough for this to brew and for me to do my morning *toilette*."

"I should do that as well."

"Would you like me to hold your coffee?"

"Not a chance. I'm taking it with me."

I hurried through cleaning my teeth, using the loo, and changing out of my bar clothes, hoping that when I finished, he'd still be on the bed.

"I hope you won't mind…" he began when I snuggled in beside him.

"Mind *what*?"

He laughed. "Rebel and Edge offered to open the Branch up tonight, in case we wanted to come in a little later."

I thought it over for a minute and realized I didn't mind. Tonight would likely be busier than even last night had been. "Not at all," I finally said when it appeared Hammer was waiting for a response.

"I'm guessing your family's pub was open seven days a week."

"There would have been riots in the streets if it wasn't."

"What about the Branch?"

"It's death for a bar if the hours change."

"I was afraid you'd say that."

"It doesn't mean you can't take time off."

"If you're there, I'm there."

"Right. Will you have to perform community service by my side as well?"

"As long as you promise not to skip bail, no."

"Why can't that be the case with the Branch?"

"Because I *want* to be there when you are." He set his coffee on the side table and turned his body so he faced me. "There are some things we need to talk about."

Feckin' hell. I hadn't even finished my first cup, and he was about to grill me. I sighed.

"Community service is one of them."

"Go on."

"It would be a good idea to get that started next week if possible."

"I suppose that's more up to you than me. But, yes, I will."

"I took a look at the judge's orders, and the number of hours stated is too high."

"I thought you'd said he wouldn't negotiate the time."

"Be right back."

"If you're getting more coffee, I'll take another cup," I said before realizing his still sat on the table. "Or I can get it."

Hammer grabbed my cup and took it with him when he left the room. When he came back, he had a computer along with a steaming refill for me.

While I sipped, he opened his laptop and brought something up on the screen. "See here? That says a total of five hundred hours."

"That is less than I anticipated."

"Right. Except, the bench warrants are for the unpaid speeding tickets, which is double-dipping."

"Isn't that the judge's prerogative?"

"Not so much. He said one hundred hours per charge. A warrant is just that; it isn't a charge."

"There's always the chance he'll raise it if I complain."

"I'll approach the DA first and see what he has to say."

"Well, then, somewhere between three and five hundred hours."

"And the fines. We should take care of those on Monday."

"We?"

"I'm still your attorney, Dublin."

"Don't remind me. I thought maybe since we slept together, you were going to tell me you found someone else to represent me."

"The day I'm not your attorney anymore, you'll know it."

I smiled, and so did he.

"Listen, I want to be serious for a moment. I know you said you were on retainer, but I'd feel so much better if I paid for your services on my behalf."

"That would be double-dipping on my part."

"Just don't bill whoever it is or whatever it is you do."

"Let's not worry about that just yet."

"Hammer!"

"Okay, I'll explain why."

"Go on."

"You know what happened with the ABT before?"

"Not the specifics. Do I need to know them?"

"Not necessarily. The main thing is the firm who has me on retainer was contracted to help infiltrate the organization in what became a nationwide sting."

"Wow. I thought it had something to do with Rebel."

"It did. She was accused of murdering one of the members. We later learned someone from the head organization had made arrangements to frame her for it. Anyway, the point is, there is some 'unfinished' business with them, so that particular 'case' is still open."

"Why'd you say it like that?"

"Well, it isn't really a case. It's more of a mission."

"*Right*. Which means my brother is involved."

"Correct."

I thought over what he'd said. To me, it seemed like a stretch that my legal issues would fall under that umbrella.

"If there was a nationwide sting, why is the case…err…mission still open…or active?"

"Because we still don't know who killed the guy Rebel was accused of murdering."

God, this was bad. No wonder my brother told me I shouldn't buy the Long Branch. Not that even this would sway me.

"I know what you're thinking."

I turned to face him. "You do?"

"There's more I need to tell you."

"That wasn't what I was thinking," I said with a wink.

"The man in the bar last night—"

I groaned. *Now* the inquisition would begin.

"You need to hear this, Maeve."

"Go on," I repeated.

"We were able to identify him via facial recognition. His name is Dion McGregor, and he is affiliated with the Westies. They're a crime syndicate operating as an offshoot of the Irish mob, albeit not with their authorization. In fact, they've attempted to wipe out their US counterparts on several occasions."

"*Feckin'* hell," I mumbled. If this McGregor was associated with this so-called crime syndicate, Cormac

Moran probably was as well. Which meant getting back what he stole from me may prove harder than I'd originally thought. Odd, though, that when Hammer said the man's name, I still had no recollection of it.

"These are known associates of McGregor's," he said, turning the screen so I could see it.

There, just to the right of the other man, was a photo of Cormac, except according to the caption beside it, his name was Daniel Gallagher.

"Recognize anyone?"

I met Hammer's gaze. He'd know straightaway if I lied. Four days ago, I'd made the decision to share my affiliation with Mary Donoghue's not just to him but to his friends. The stakes were much higher this time. I'd not told a soul about my pursuit of Moran, aka Gallagher, nor did anyone other than me know what he stole. Not even Kellen.

"Maeve?"

I took a deep breath, raised my hand, and pointed to the screen. "Him."

"Is that the ex?"

"Aye."

Hammer set the computer to the side and pulled me into his arms. It was literally the last thing I'd anticipated and nearly spilled what was left of my coffee.

"I know how hard that was for you."

I squeezed my eyes closed when I felt tears of relief fill them. I'd not expected that to happen either. There was still so much I hadn't told him. I'd really not told him anything, but like when I confessed what happened when I shot Bobby, getting started was the hardest part.

"I knew him as Cormac Moran."

Rather than let go so I could say more, Hammer held me tighter.

17

Hammer

I witnessed Maeve's inner turmoil as she'd studied the images on the screen. Without her pointing to him, I already knew—by her facial expressions alone—which man was her ex. That she summoned the courage to tell me, trusted me enough, meant so much to me. Without thinking, I'd grabbed her and pulled her into my arms. Rather than stiffen, she settled into my embrace in the same way she had last night. And that meant I was in big trouble.

Last night after I was certain Maeve was asleep, I'd eased out from under her and went to get my laptop. While there was nothing yet from Decker on the mystery man's ID, probably since it was still the middle of the night, there was someone else I wanted to look for. I just didn't know who yet.

I'd scrolled through the bar listings of lawyers practicing in Austin. Given it was the state capital, there were several hundred, and yet, I couldn't identify a single one I'd trust to represent the woman I wanted to sleep next to from this night on, for as long as she'd let me.

One person came to mind this morning, but I had no idea if she was currently practicing, and if she was, where. Decker would know, and later today, I'd message him and ask.

"Hammer?"

"Yeah?"

When she didn't say anything, I eased my arms from around her, and she sat up.

"What is this?" She motioned with her hand from me to her. "I mean…you're still my lawyer."

I rubbed the top of my head. "I am."

"So…"

"So I'm confusing you."

"I'd say."

I smiled. "I'm sorry about that, but I'm not sorry you fell asleep in my arms."

Maeve twisted away and sat on the edge of the bed. "This is so different for me. I haven't felt this way…" She looked over her shoulder. "I mean, don't worry; I'm not falling in love or anything as ridiculous as that. It's more that I haven't felt a physical attraction to anyone in longer than I care to admit."

Why had I felt a twinge of pain in my chest when Maeve said she wasn't falling in love? I certainly wasn't, either. As she'd said, it was ridiculous. It would sound trite if I admitted I hadn't felt a physical attraction in longer than I cared to admit too, so I kept quiet.

"I'm working on it."

She turned her body and rested against the headboard like I was. "On what?"

"Finding you another lawyer."

Her eyes opened wide. "What will you tell Kellen?"

I chuckled. "I haven't figured that out yet."

"Who's the lawyer?"

"To be honest, I'm not sure about that either."

"But you're working on it?"

"That's right."

"Why?"

My gaze went from her eyes to her lips. "Because I can't stop myself from doing this." I grasped the back of her neck and kissed her. When she put her hands on my shoulders, pulled me closer, and whimpered, it ignited a passion in me more intense than anything I'd ever felt. I had to have this woman. Not just physically. My need to possess her in every way was all-encompassing. I wanted to crawl inside her body, her mind, her soul, keep every part of her safe and protected.

I broke the kiss and stared into her eyes, knowing that what I wanted from her and who she was, were in fundamental opposition.

She was independent and trusted no one, even when she was left with no choice but to. Trying to possess her would be akin to keeping an eagle in a birdcage, wings clipped, spirit devastated.

I couldn't do that to her or to me. When I let go of her physically, it felt like I had completely.

"What just happened?" she asked, eyes wide, lip trembling.

I sighed. "You and I are in such different places in life. I'm not sure I've ever been where you are, and so much of me wishes I had."

She rolled off the bed. "What in the bloody hell does that even mean?"

"It means I wish I was more like you."

She studied me, maybe to discern whether I was lying. Finally, she sat back down. "You're convinced you're too mature for me."

I smiled that she'd said mature versus old because it wasn't about age. "Too stodgy for you."

"And I'm too immature for you."

"I would gladly spend the rest of my life orbiting the wonder of you."

"But?"

"I fear that's the most I can do."

"You're making the decision for both of us, then? No opportunity for me to share my thoughts or feelings? If that's the case, you're right. You can remain a spectator."

She got off the bed and left me alone in the room and with my thoughts. So fucking wise beyond her years. Or maybe she was just so much wiser than me.

Rather than follow her, I called Decker.

"Hey, Hammer. I was just getting ready to call you."

"What about?"

"I've got eyes on McGregor. He's up to something."

"Meaning?"

"He's been asking around about certain members of the ABT. Not only that. He's recently moved into the Westies' number-two position."

"Let me guess, second only to Gallagher."

"Bingo."

"Listen, there was another reason I called you. Do you know what Ellison Storm is up to these days?"

"Fury? As a matter of fact, I do."

I chuckled to myself. There were few code names as appropriately given as hers had been. Maybe she wasn't the best choice to take over as Maeve's attorney. The two might butt heads worse than she and I did. "Anything you can tell me?"

"Tell me why you're asking first."

"Last I heard, she was getting ready to hang her shingle." The term was antiquated, but then so were Deck and I.

"Passed the bar last year."

"Do you know where she's practicing?"

"Last I heard was Houston. I don't think she's settled into any firm yet. You still haven't told me why you want to know."

"I'm thinking about finding McTiernan different representation."

Decker was quiet long enough that it worried me.

"Nothing to say?" I finally asked.

"One thing I know about you, Hammer, is you're not impulsive."

"Are you saying this is out of character?"

"No. If that's what I was saying, that's what I would've said."

I laughed. It was exactly the kind of thing known to come out of my mouth.

"I may be stepping over the line with what I'm about to say, but you and I have been friends most of our lives, so I'm going to say it anyway."

This was where Decker told me to get back to thinking with the brain in my head rather than the one in my pants. It was something I'd already told myself a thousand times.

"I've been where you are, and I almost lost Mila because of it. Don't make the same mistakes I did."

It was a good thing I was sitting down, because that's how much his words stunned me.

"If there's something there, between you and Maeve, offer Fury whatever it'll take to get her down here. Hell, offer her a partnership in your practice. Wouldn't be anyone better to take some of the load off your shoulders, at least for the Invincibles. I doubt you have time for any other clients." He cleared his throat. "You still there, Hammer?"

"I am."

"Good, I would hate to have to repeat all that, given how eloquently it came out the first time."

I laughed out loud. This was why I valued my friendship with him as much as I did. He never hesitated to say what he thought.

"I appreciate the advice." Especially since it spoke directly to what Maeve had said to me a few minutes earlier. I had made a decision for both of us.

"Heed it, or you'll regret it. And, Hammer? Do not wait. That's what almost cost me the love of my life. Look at us now."

His situation was enviable, no question about that. Deck and his wife were living and raising their family on a ranch that bordered the King-Alexander spread.

"While I was waxing so poetically, I sent a message to Fury. She's expecting your call."

"Thanks, Deck."

"You heard me about not hesitating, right, boy?"

I laughed again. I was older than the man who'd just called me "boy."

"Roger that, sir."

When I hung up, I saw Deck had sent Fury's number in a message.

"Hammer, it's nice to hear from you," she said when she picked up.

"How are you, Fury?"

"Fierce as ever. I hear you might have a job for me."

Whether it worked out that Ellison took over Maeve's representation or not, I was certainly ready to relinquish some of the work I did on behalf of the Invincibles. Her career began at the CIA, working for Money McTiernan, as a matter of fact. Once she left the agency, she became a contract operative and finally a lawyer. That meant as a candidate, she checked every box.

"When can we meet?" she asked.

"How soon can you get here?"

"If I leave now, I'll be there before sundown."

"We're at the new house. See you then."

My next order of business was finding Maeve, bringing her up to speed, and praying the two women hit it off.

I found her in the room where she'd told me to put a piano, staring out the window. Keeping Decker's advice in mind, I walked over, spun her around, and kissed her the way I should've before. So she knew without question that before the day ended, I wouldn't be her lawyer anymore—I was counting on it.

Rather than feeling like I was doing something wrong or telling myself I needed to stop, I kissed

Maeve with every ounce of passion I felt for her. Our tongues danced, our lips pressed hard, our teeth nibbled. I put both hands on her ass, and she wound her legs around my waist. I could feel her heat and wetness through the thin layer of sweats I'd changed into when I got up in the middle of the night, and she could feel how hard I was for her.

Every whimper, every moan was like a siren's song, urging me to take more, and I did. Our mouths still fused together, I carried her up the stairs and over to the bed where we'd slept the night before.

I lay her on her back, reached under, and pulled her yoga pants and panties right off. Maeve assisted by doing the same with her sweatshirt. All of which landed in a pile on the floor. I gripped her hips and lowered my head, inhaling the intoxicating scent of her pussy, but before I took a taste, Maeve put her hands on my shoulders and pushed.

"I need to see you naked too."

We repeated similar motions. Maeve pulled down my sweats and boxer briefs while I took off my shirt.

"God Almighty," she moaned, running her hands down the front of my body, starting with my shoulders straight down to my cock that was so hard it pulsed.

When she wrapped her hands around me and leaned forward to lick the tip, I did what she'd done to me. I pushed her shoulders until she was flat on her back and settled between her thighs.

With one swoop of my tongue, I licked through her exquisite folds while one hand teased her nipple and the fingers of the other toyed with her clit.

I eased one of those fingers inside her wet heat while my mouth sucked.

"Hammer…God…"

I increased my efforts, adding a second finger and sucking harder, all the while keeping my eyes fixated on hers. When she came for the first time by my hand and mouth, I wanted to see, feel, experience every moment of it.

She curled her body up, wove her fingers in my hair, and exploded on my tongue.

18

Maeve

While I'd orgasmed by my own hand only a few days ago, I couldn't remember the last time I did before that. Long before things ended with Cormac—or whatever the bastard's name was. As far as lovers went, he wasn't very apt, even though he believed himself a master of it. Seduction, yes. Pleasure, not so much.

Hammer was another story entirely. Since the first time we touched, my body had been burning for his. It was only sheer and utter exhaustion that had kept me from taking what I wanted from him last night, and I wanted everything from this man.

"My turn," I said, pushing him onto the floor. I straddled him and ran my hands over his pecs, tracing the words of his tattoo with the nail of my index finger, this time with more pressure than the first time I'd done it. He gasped, closed his eyes, and arched his neck. He *liked* it, which meant I did too. I shifted backwards, dragging my wet pussy over his skin, his shaft, his thighs. There, I stopped, took him in my hands, and stroked. *Slowly.* Punishing him for how long he'd made me wait for this.

I lowered my body so my nipples tickled his pelvis at the same time I lowered my mouth, taking him deep enough that he cried out my name. I slowly eased off before repeating the same motion.

Like I did with him, Hammer held my head, as if he had a prayer of controlling what I did to him. I laughed from somewhere deep in my chest. The vibration alone made him pulsate in my mouth.

He opened his eyes and looked into mine, just like he had when he'd been pleasuring me. "Put me inside you."

I shook my head and circled his cock with my tongue.

"Please," he groaned. "I'm begging."

"I can't do that."

His eyes scrunched. "Why in God's name not?"

"I can't reach a condom from here."

Hammer raised his head. "You have one? Where is it?"

"In my bag. I'll get it if you promise not to move."

He nodded.

"Not even your little finger."

"I won't even blink."

I climbed off, reached for my bag, and grabbed the string of packets I'd put in there when he took me to my house in Austin.

Straddling him again, I tore one open and rolled it on his cock before positioning myself so my pussy was right above it. I dragged his hardness back and forth, coating him with my wetness.

I shook my head when he put his hands on my waist, but he didn't let go. Instead, his eyes bored into mine as I slowly lowered myself.

"Holy Jesus, you feel good," Hammer said through gritted teeth.

I let my body adjust to having him inside me before lowering myself the rest of the way in one fell swoop like I had with my mouth. Hammer's eyes rolled back in his head.

He left me to my slow, languorous tease longer than I'd thought he would before rolling me onto my back and setting a rhythm that soon had me spiraling over the precipice of the most toe-curling orgasm I'd ever experienced.

I'd barely caught my breath when he gathered me in his arms and lifted me to the bed.

"I'm just getting started," he said, toying with my nipples and kissing the soft skin on the side of my torso.

For an instant, I wondered if Edge and Rebel could take over the bar all night, so Hammer and I could stay in this bed until tomorrow morning.

"What are you thinking about?" he asked, bringing his mouth to the nipple he'd been swirling his finger around.

I laughed. "I don't want to work tonight."

"I like the sound of that."

When he thrust his ready-to-go-again cock into my pussy, I forgot about work, even my own name.

I'd drifted off, but woke when Hammer's phone vibrated.

"What?" I groaned when he swiped the screen and swore.

"Your new lawyer is here."

"Are you serious?"

"She made better time than she thought."

She? Interesting. While unexpected, it pleased me.

"I'll go down and greet her. Take your time, and when you're ready, join us."

"What's her name?"

"Ellison Storm, but everyone calls her Fury."

I raised a brow. *Fury?* I liked her already. After Hammer got dressed and left the room, I went to the window and looked out in time to see a woman get out of a large sedan and look around. From this distance, she looked as though she could be related to me. Same dark hair and pale skin, similar height and weight, and when she looked up, I saw she was pretty. Given that, I'd hardly be taking my time joining them.

I didn't see them right away, but I followed the sound of laughter into the kitchen, where they were seated at the table.

"Hello," I said, approaching. Both stood.

"I'm Maeve." I held out my hand. "You're Fury, right?"

Her eyes opened wide, and she shook her head. "Nice to meet you, but damn, I feel like I'm looking in a mirror."

"You do?" asked Hammer, looking between the two of us.

"I mean, our features are different, but otherwise, someone could mistake us for being the same person."

Hammer pulled out a chair, and I took a seat, as did they.

"I've been talking with Fury about your case."

The woman nodded. "If you're comfortable with me taking over, I'll be representing you in any further court proceedings. Hammer will remain your attorney of record."

"You'll still be my attorney?" I asked, looking at him. If that were the case, what was the point of this?

"Fury will be joining my firm, so my name will remain on the case files and I'll continue to be responsible for the writ bond."

"Will you still be my attorney or *not*?"

He smiled. *"Not."*

"For the time being, Fury will be staying in the other house."

My eyes opened wide. "Which other house?"

"Mine."

"The one you originally took me to?"

"Yeah. Why?"

I looked at Fury. "I'd look for another place if I were you."

"It's okay. I've stayed there before, haven't I?" She looked across the table at Hammer and winked.

I glanced at him and wished I hadn't. He appeared embarrassed—maybe even mortified. I sat back and folded my arms. Had he really asked someone he'd had sex with to take over as my attorney?

"Did you want to discuss the other things?" Fury asked him.

"We probably should." Hammer still hadn't looked in my direction.

"Right. If you'll excuse me." He moved to help with my chair, but I'd already pushed it back and stood. "I'm going for a walk."

"Stay out of the bull pasture."

I didn't bother to turn around and look at him. If I had, he would've seen the *fury* on my face. Not only was the woman who would be my new attorney either a current or former lover of his, but he'd just embarrassed me in front of her.

I suppose it stood to reason that he was attracted to her, given she was practically my body double. Apparently, the man had a type.

"Where are you off to?" asked Rip, who rode up on a horse at the same time I rushed out the front door.

"I need some fresh air."

"I heard Fury is here."

Evidently, by the look on his face, she was his type too.

"Feckin' eejits," I muttered before I walked past him.

"Hey, wait. It'll be dark soon. You probably don't wanna be walking out here by yourself."

"Why not? Isn't it safe?"

"No tellin' what kind of critters you might run into."

"Bloody hell," I muttered under my breath. "Are you going to the Branch tonight?"

"Yep. I should actually be heading over there in the next hour or so."

"Can you give me a lift?"

He hesitated.

"Hammer is still meeting with the attorney."

"I should probably let him know."

When he pulled out his phone, I wanted to shoot it out of his hand, not that I had my gun.

"Damn cell coverage. Works in the house, but not out here." He dismounted from the horse. "Be right back, then we'll leave," he said before going in the front door.

As if I would wait. I hurried over to my pickup and breathed a sigh of relief when I found he'd returned the key to where I always kept it. I was more than halfway down the driveway before I saw someone come out the front door. It could've been Rip or Hammer; the two looked enough alike. Like *Fury* and I did.

Rather than go to the bar, I went in the direction of the city.

19

Hammer

"Sorry to interrupt. I'm heading to the Branch now."

I wondered why Rip felt the need to keep me abreast of his schedule until I realized he hadn't come in to talk to me.

He took off his cowboy hat. "Hey, Fury. How've you been?"

"Good, Rip, you?"

"Good, too. Thanks."

The last time I'd seen these two together was when I came home from a mission a day early and found them not just in my house, but making good use of my bed. I decided to excuse myself.

"Hey, Rip. Can you let Edge and Rebel know Maeve and I will be there within the hour?" I pushed back my chair and stood.

"Actually, she asked if I could give her a lift since you were in a meeting."

What the hell? She said she was going for a walk. "We're finished. I'll take her." I looked between the two people who might as well be the only ones in the room. "You guys catch up."

I left the kitchen and went upstairs to change, but I didn't see Maeve. Where was she?

I asked Rip that very question when I came back downstairs and found him still in the kitchen with Fury.

"Oh, shit. She's waitin' on me. Sorry, Hammer."

I went out the front door, and Rip followed.

"She was right here. Maybe she decided to go for a walk, after all. Wait. *Oh, shit,*" he repeated.

I followed his line of sight. Her pickup was gone. "Tell me you didn't leave the keys in it."

"Not in it."

"Jesus. You put them back where she keeps them, didn't you?" I didn't expect an answer, and Rip didn't give one. Maybe because I already had my phone out.

When my call to her cell went straight to voicemail, I called the Branch. "Hey, Rebel. Did Maeve show up yet?"

"I haven't seen her come in. Hang on, and I'll ask Edge." She set the phone down while I counted the seconds. "Nope, he hasn't seen her, either. You aren't comin' in with her tonight?"

"No, I am. She just left before me, and I wanted to ask her something."

"Well, I'm sure she'll be here shortly. The Branch isn't that far from your place."

"Right. Thanks, Rebel. Shoot me a text if she gets there before I do."

"Will do, Hammer. Gotta run. This place is packed."

"Yep. See ya soon."

"What are you thinkin'?" Rip asked.

I didn't know what to think. Given the afternoon we'd had, I expected her to be happier than she appeared when she left to let Fury and I talk about a possible role with the Invincibles. But why would she just leave without telling me? "How did she seem when you talked to her?"

"Seemed okay. Anxious to get to the Branch."

"Okay. I'll head there now."

"Right behind ya, boss."

I called her cell again before I started the engine. Straight to voicemail.

Something didn't feel right. Why would she leave without telling me? When I'd jokingly asked if she'd still want to have sex with me once it was no longer forbidden, I didn't expect it to happen this fast. Was she embarrassed? No. That didn't make sense. First of all, she seemed as satisfied as I'd been this afternoon. Second, Maeve wasn't the type to hide her tail between her legs.

When I pulled into the Long Branch parking lot, I saw that, like Rebel had said, the place was packed. I drove around for a couple of minutes. There were plenty of old pickups, and since I hadn't really paid attention to the details of hers, I couldn't tell if it was one of them or not.

I parked, went inside, and made my way through the crowd and over to the end of the bar.

"Hey, Hammer," said Rebel.

"Is she here?"

"I haven't seen her, but she could've sneaked in. We've been completely slammed."

While I'd seen nights where Bobby and one other bartender could handle the crowd easily, tonight Rebel had three other guys pouring with her, and they were having a hard time keeping up. I couldn't jump in, though. I had to figure out where in the hell Maeve was.

I stalked into the back room and over to the office. The door was locked. I pounded on it, but since it didn't look like there was a light on, I figured Maeve wasn't inside. I was almost back to the bar when Rip met me. "Is she here?"

I shook my head. I called her a third time, but the same thing happened. "Straight to voicemail," I muttered.

"Where else would she go?"

The only place I could think of was her house in Austin. "Maybe home. I'll head there now. If you see her, let me know immediately."

"Roger that, boss."

What in the hell had happened that would make her take off? Nothing made sense. On the drive to Austin, I went from worried to pissed and back to worried. Even though I didn't expect different results, I kept calling her cell.

I thought about calling Money to see if he'd heard from her, but if he hadn't, it would only make him as worried as I was. Plus, if he had, he probably would've called me to intervene on her behalf for whatever had made her leave.

I pulled into the driveway, disappointed when I didn't see a truck and the place looked dark. I got out of the Porsche anyway and rang the doorbell. Like before, all the blinds were down, so I couldn't see inside, but I walked around the house to see if any of the other rooms appeared lit up. None did.

Not knowing what else to do, I called her brother.

"Hey, Hammer. What's up?" It sounded as though I woke him.

"Have you heard from your sister?"

"Not since the last time we talked. *Why?*"

"She took off in her truck. I thought she'd gone to the bar, but she wasn't there. She isn't home either."

"What happened?"

"If you mean why did she leave, I have no idea. I was finishing up a meeting with Fury, and we were supposed to go to the Branch together."

"Nothing my sister does surprises me."

"Do you have any idea where she might've gone?"

"Back to Ireland?"

It was the only other possibility I could think of. "Thanks, Money. I'll keep you posted."

"Hold up a sec. According to the last ping from her phone, she's at home. Are you sure she's not there?"

"As sure as I can be. Didn't answer the door, and the place is dark. I tried to call her several times, but it's gone straight to voicemail."

"The door code is 627962383."

I told him I'd get back to him, smiling as I punched the code onto the keypad and realized the letters the numbers represented. *MaryMaeve.*

"Maeve?" I called out. "It's Hammer. I'm coming in."

No response. I checked every room. There was no sign of a struggle. No sign of her phone either. I called it again, but like it had so many other times before, it went straight to voicemail.

Rather than call, I sent Money a text confirming she wasn't there before getting in my car, moving it a couple of blocks over, and returning to her house to wait. If she was mad—for some unknown fucking reason—came home, and saw my car, she might decide to go somewhere else.

"Sorry to bother you, Decker," I said when he answered my call. "I need your help."

"Shoot."

"Maeve McTiernan's gone missing. I called Money to see if he'd heard from her, and he hasn't. He's afraid she might be headed back to Ireland."

"On it. Where are you now?"

"At her place in the city."

"I'll be in touch if I have anything to report."

I sent a text to Rip, even though I knew damn well I would've heard from him if Maeve had shown up.

"Hey, Fury, are you still at my new place?" I asked when she picked up.

"No, I'm on my way to the bar. I haven't eaten, and I could go for a nice T-bone. What's up?"

"I was just wondering if Maeve returned."

"Returned?"

I realized I hadn't told her new attorney that Maeve appeared to have vanished, and I doubted Rip had, either. "Yeah, I'm not sure where she is."

"Where are you?"

"At her house."

"Do you want me to go back to the ranch?"

"Might be a good idea. I know it isn't a T-bone, but there is food there."

"That's okay. I'd only be able to eat a quarter of it anyway. Let me know if there's something else you want me to do."

"Copy that." Something occurred to me, and I called Rip.

"Nothing yet," he said.

"Who's at the ranch and can check the security cameras?"

"Pete's there."

"Have him make sure she actually left."

"Roger that."

"And, Rip, figure out all the routes that would take her from the ranch to the bar."

"There's only one, Hammer. Unless she went off-roading, and that ol' truck wouldn't have made it ten feet."

"Have a couple of the other guys drive it real slow."

While I didn't notice a truck off the side of the road earlier, I hadn't been looking. There was the chance she'd gone into a ditch, but then why would Money have said the phone pinged from her house?

"Anything else?"

"Not right now, but I'm sure I'll think of something as soon as we end this call."

"Copy that. You still in Austin?"

"Yeah, but I'll head back soon."

I hung up, racking my brain and trying to figure out where in the hell Maeve would've gone. I called Decker a second time.

"Nothin' yet," he said.

"Do you have a known address for either Dion McGregor or Daniel Gallagher?"

"Woulda led with that if I did, but I'll take another look."

"Is there someone else you can stake out at her place?"

"Affirmative. I'll get Jagger on it. I'm checking airports now."

While I waited to hear back from him, I pulled up the photos of the two men he'd sent me. I walked the two blocks to my car and drove to one of the places where I knew the ABT hung out.

It was two in the morning by the time I'd exhausted every idea I had about where Maeve might have gone. I was no longer pissed. Now, all I felt was worry. On my way out of Austin, I called Rip.

"Any luck, boss?"

"*Nada.* You need any help closing up?"

"No, we're leavin' soon."

"I think we need to consider Maeve is missing rather than has jumped bail. See who you can gather."

"Where do you want us?"

"The new house."

For now, my spread would serve as the best option for a command center. It made sense, given someone would be there in the event Maeve returned.

Rip called back a few minutes later to report Edge and Decker were on their way. Ink and Rage were too.

Once I got home and unintentionally woke Fury, who'd been asleep on my couch, I tried to convince her to go upstairs, to the guest room.

"Fill me in."

I briefed her more on what I hadn't found rather than had, rattled off the list of people Rip said were on their way here, and told her I'd update her on the rest after she'd gotten some sleep.

"I'm part of the team again, Hammer. The last thing I'd do is sleep."

Ink, Rage, and Rip arrived first. Edge was next, probably because he'd dropped Rebel off at home. Decker was right behind him. For now, with the addition of Fury and me, those gathered made up the team. Plenty of other partners or contractors would be on the first flight out if they knew I needed help.

"Here's what we know," began Decker. "Maeve never arrived at the Long Branch tonight. We believe she went to her place in Austin, because that's where her phone was last tracked to. However, Hammer confirmed she wasn't there. Suspecting she might try to return to Ireland, I checked footage at Austin-Bergstrom, San Antonio, George Bush, DFW, and Corpus Christi airports. No sign of her. Any questions so far?"

No one spoke up.

Deck looked over at me before continuing. "You were right to assume she went in the direction of Austin. I was able to get a hold of tonight's footage from the Quickstop at the corner, and she made a right rather than a left."

A left would've taken her to the bar. A right, just about anywhere else.

"Tomorrow, I'll see about gathering security footage from the places along the route."

"I can help with that," offered Rip.

"Ink and Rage, you get with Rip and divide and conquer."

"You hearin' anything from inside the ABT?" Deck asked.

"We have someone on the inside?"

"Have for a few months," said Edge.

That was news to me, but I wasn't usually on that side of the operation. It was only after one of the team got in some kind of trouble or needed legal advice that I was called in.

"And to answer your question, I haven't. Our guy is in deep, and communication has been too risky. I'm stepping up the efforts to contact him now."

"What about the Westies?" I asked.

"Not with them, but with the Family, we do."

The Irish crime syndicate, known simply that way, had achieved exponential growth while Irish law enforcement's resources were stretched thin by the Kinahan and Byrnes gangs.

Given the collective Irish Mafia—which included all three of those organizations plus many more—was adamant that there would be no sanctioned affiliations outside of the country, the Westies were more adversaries than allies. Which worked in our favor.

"Edge will work with our sources to find out what he can about McGregor and Gallagher."

"What do we do now?" I pleaded as much as asked. I felt powerless, not something I was accustomed to.

"I think it's time to alert Money."

It was four on the East Coast, but I knew Money would be up—if he'd ever gone to sleep.

"Decker," Money answered on the first ring, letting me know I was right to think he hadn't slept.

"I'm puttin' you on speakerphone." He ran down the list of who was in the room.

I could hear the relief in McTiernan's voice. If Deck were calling with bad news, he never would've suggested anyone else be part of the conversation.

"What have you discovered?" Money asked.

"She left the ranch at approximately seven last night. Every sign was that she was headed to the Long Branch. However, she never arrived. I haven't been able to check much security footage, but what I have seen indicates that when your sister left here, she went in the opposite direction of the bar. Hammer confirmed she wasn't home after you traced her phone to that location. We do have eyes on the place in case she shows up."

"Copy that," Money responded.

"I think it's time for you to come to Texas," I said, meeting Deck's eyes. He nodded.

"On my way. How much more support do you want to come with me?"

"None for now," answered Deck. "I'm pulling in more from our team."

"Thanks. It'll get me there quicker. And so you don't have to, I'll address the elephant in the room. We have two primary suspects if my sister has been abducted—the Westies and the ABT. If you haven't already, I'd get set up to trace a ransom call."

"It's in place," said Decker. "Oh, and Money, the Invincibles' plane is at Dulles. Flight plan filed. Pilots are on standby."

"I'll head there now."

"Who else are you thinking of bringing in on this?" I asked Decker once the call ended with Money.

"Jagger has Shredder and Steel on standby if we need them."

"Steel? The bouncer?"

"One and the same," answered Edge. "We brought him in last year."

"Copy that."

If Maeve had been taken against her will, Money's suspicion of the Westies and the ABT was a sentiment shared by the rest of us in the room. I was leaning more toward the former, given the man who'd recently been named the leader of the gang was well aware of Maeve's wealth. Couple that with his number two showing up at the Long Branch, and it put them at the top of the list, as far as I was concerned.

The ABT would have a different agenda, although money would likely be their end goal.

When Edge went into the kitchen, I followed. As he'd just alluded to, it had been one year since the Invincibles' last run-in with the ABT. Then, Rebel had been attacked in retaliation for the death of a member. It had occurred outside of an Austin restaurant where she was working, and it didn't seem to matter that she hadn't killed the guy they called Possum; they still blamed her for his death.

While the prevailing belief among those involved on our side was that someone in the national organization—Aryan Nation—had put a hit on the guy, the murder itself still hadn't been solved.

"I want to ask you something," I said to Edge when he poured himself a cup of coffee.

"About?"

"Have you gotten any closer to figuring out who killed Possum?"

Edge sneered. "I hope that bloody bastard is in the depths of hell, but to answer your question, nothing concrete."

"Any theories?"

"A recent one, in fact." He motioned with his head, and I followed him into the main dining room, where folding tables and chairs had been set up without my realizing it had happened.

"This guy." Edge pulled up the photos of Dion MacGregor and Daniel Gallagher and pointed to the one on the right—Maeve's ex. "There's something familiar about him."

"Seen him around? Maybe at the Branch?"

Edge shook his head.

"What makes you think he has something to do with Possum's death?"

"Gut."

That was as good a reason as any other and what we'd all learned to trust during our Special Forces training. Gut and instinct—they were as important as the guns we carried.

I found my jacket where I'd thrown it on a chair in what I now considered the piano room, even though it didn't have one. Yet. And I'd be damned if I didn't find Maeve and have her pick one out with me. I grabbed the pocket humidor and pulled out a stogie.

"Where's Hammer?" I heard Deck holler.

"Here." I met him in the foyer.

"We got a hit on the truck, but still no sign of Maeve."

20

Maeve

"For the last *feckin'* time, I don't know where Gallagher is, and if I did, I would've killed the bastard long before you came along."

The two arseholes lying in wait at my house when I arrived must've been tipped off that I was headed there since neither of them seemed smart enough to plan a damn thing. No, these two were brawn. I needed to speak with someone who had a brain.

The apartment they were holding me in didn't belong to either of them. Having looked at one in the luxury high-rise when I first arrived in Austin, I knew it was far above their pay grade.

"Tell your boss I'll speak with no one but him."

They looked at each other before the bigger of the two said, "You'll talk to us or no one."

"Are you sure about that? Maybe you should check."

They looked at each other *again*. Lord in heaven, even I could teach these two how to be better criminals.

"While you decide, I need to use the loo."

Zig turned to Zag, who didn't appear to have any idea what I was talking about.

"The facilities? The ladies' room? A toilet?"

The smaller man untied the rope binding me to the chair, grabbed my arm, and pulled me into the hallway. He opened a door and pushed me inside. "Make it quick."

"Tough to make it at all if you don't untie me." I turned my back to him and waved the fingers of my bound hands. He looked over his shoulder, but as I'd anticipated, his counterpart must've been using the opportunity to get in contact with someone higher up.

He sighed and used a knife to cut the twine. *Eejit.* It would take me less than ten seconds to knee him in the balls while I used one hand to chop his arm and grabbed the knife with the other. I might have done it if he and I were alone, but we weren't. Besides, I was ready to make a deal with whoever ordered this half-arsed kidnapping.

As I suspected, dumb, dumber, and I hadn't been alone in the apartment. Either that, or the man seated in a chair when I came out of the loo had arrived quite quickly.

"Who are you?" I demanded when the one who'd cut the twine off my wrists retied them, pulled me over to the same dining chair I'd been seated in previously, and bound me to it.

The new arrival didn't respond but had a black look in his eyes, the way all truly bad boys did. He wasn't just bad; he was dangerous. Dark, spiked hair, green eyes, and more facial hair than Hammer, just not the full beard I'd grown to detest, made him look almost devilish.

The man's shoulders were broad and his hands strong. Powerful enough to snap my neck with his thick fingers.

He looked lean yet muscled under his dress shirt, and while the material of his trousers strained against his legs, it wasn't as taut as Hammer's. I found myself comparing everything about him to my former attorney. With him, I'd felt an immediate attraction so intense there was no denying it.

"Leave us," the man said in an American accent I didn't recognize. It wasn't Texan nor from New York City, yet it seemed distinct. Not Southern either.

"Where are you from?" I asked.

When he sneered, I noticed his teeth were perfectly straight and almost blindingly white. Once the other two *eejits* left the room, he stood, approached, and pulled out one of the other dining chairs. He moved it close enough that when he sat, my legs were between his spread ones. I expected him to touch me, but he didn't.

"They said you were beautiful."

I raised my chin. "Do you disagree?"

He shook his head. "You're beyond that."

"Compliments will only get you somewhere if you untie me."

"Hmm." He studied me. "Obvious what Daniel sees in you, but is it enough to get him to come for you, I wonder?"

I sneered like he had. "Come for me? He's hiding from me."

"Lovers' spat?"

"I'd ask the same of you."

"You're amusing." He leaned forward as if he intended to touch my cheek, but dropped his hand.

My eyes scrunched. "Why do you want to find him?"

"He took something of mine."

I nodded. "Aye. I've the same reason."

"I've heard you're quite clever."

"You didn't hear that from Cormac."

He raised a brow.

"Cormac Moran, aka Daniel Gallagher, is the lowest form of life on the planet. So low that he doesn't deserve to breathe air he doesn't believe anyone else is entitled to."

"Are you saying you intend to kill him?"

"Once I've gotten back what's mine."

"Is he worth going to prison over, Mary Maeve?"

I tried not to react to his letting on he knew exactly who I was. "What makes you think anyone would care?"

He scooted the chair back, stood, and walked over to the windows. "I don't believe you'd do it."

"Then you're not adept at knowing the truth from a lie."

"Is that a skill of yours?"

"It became one because of the man you call Gallagher."

"You told my men you wouldn't speak to anyone but me. Is this all you had to say?"

I shook my head. "Certainly not. I'm prepared to offer you a deal."

21

Hammer

"Found the truck parked off South Congress. Rip confirmed it's hers. I'm working on area security footage now."

"Who found it?" I asked Decker.

"Steel. He lives in the neighborhood and noticed it on his way home after work. Not too many vehicles parked in the permit-only zones after the bars close."

"The restaurant where he works, do they have security cameras?"

"Steel is gathering those now, then he'll head this way."

"Tell him not to."

Decker looked up from his computer. "Why not?"

"I'll go to him."

"Me too," said Edge.

"Copy that. I'll tell Steel to engage Shredder. Hammer, anyone else you want to go with you?"

"Not for now." Rip, Ink, and Rage would be of better service staying here to help Decker collect security footage along the route Maeve took into Austin. Fury could also stay here and help Decker with whatever else he needed.

With so many of us who had been helping at the Branch pulled in on this instead, I wondered if we should close tomorrow night. Sunday would be a helluva lot easier for customers to understand than if we'd done it on a Friday or Saturday. It was something I'd discuss with Edge on our way to Austin.

"We'll meet at Steel's place," Edge said once we were in his SUV. He turned to look at me. "You doin' okay, Hammer?"

"Fuck no." I rubbed my head. "Maeve was my responsibility. Not just to make sure she didn't jump bail. It was my responsibility to keep her safe too."

"I've known you a long time."

"And?"

"There's more to it."

I didn't want to discuss this with Edge. I didn't want to discuss it with anyone. What was between Maeve and me—not just the sex, all of it—was something I wanted to hold close for now. "Maybe," I muttered.

"If you change your mind and want to talk about it, I'm here."

"Appreciate that, man."

I told him what I'd been thinking as far as closing the Branch tomorrow.

"Sundays are pretty slow. Rebel can handle it with Bobby's employees. The bouncers know to be on the lookout for the ABT as well as anyone else MacIver has previously banned. Tres knows to contact Mac if he needs backup."

"Do you think we should read the sheriff in on this?"

"Not yet."

When we got to Steel's place and went inside, he said he'd reviewed the restaurant's security footage, and it didn't cover the area where the truck was parked, nor was there any video of someone driving it on South Congress.

"I know all the owners or managers of every place in this section of the neighborhood. A little later this morning, I can start contacting the retail shops. Some of the restaurants open for breakfast and lunch too."

"Where is the truck?" Edge asked.

"Couple blocks over."

"This wasn't here before," said Steel. He took a parking ticket from under the wiper blade after leading us to where the vehicle was parked. "At least they haven't towed it."

It took Edge all of thirty seconds to get into the old truck to dust for prints as well as look for clues as to what may have happened. There were two full prints—likely Maeve's and Rip's—and one partial. "Whoever parked the truck here attempted to clean the evidence, just not very effectively."

Criminals, especially the types who ended up in street gangs, wouldn't ever be considered geniuses.

"What's this?" I heard him say, reaching between the seat cushions. He held up a cell phone I recognized as Maeve's. "It's dead," he said before bagging it.

It must've died right after she arrived at her place, which is why it'd pinged there and nowhere else.

"There's not much more we can do until later this morning," Edge said on the way back to Steel's place.

"Right." I couldn't just go back to the ranch, though. I had to do something, or I'd go crazy. "I'd like to go back to Maeve's house and do a more thorough search."

"Let us know if you find footage of someone parking the truck," Edge said to Steel before we returned to his SUV.

"Maeve lives in Hyde Park," I said, realizing then that he probably already had the address entered into the GPS.

"I don't miss spending time here," he said as we drove through Austin.

"No?"

Edge continued talking, but I wasn't listening. Was Maeve somewhere in this city, maybe inside any number of the buildings we drove past? Was she hurt? As Money had suggested, would a ransom call be coming in, and if so, to whom?

She'd been gone almost twelve hours. In that time, she could easily have been transported across the border into Mexico. The possible scenarios were endless. Running through them would make me crazy.

I rested my head against the back of the seat and closed my eyes, but not because I wanted to sleep. Instead, I let my mind rewind to yesterday afternoon and how Maeve's body had felt against mine, how it felt to kiss her, to hold her in my arms, to witness the look on her face as I brought her to orgasm after orgasm.

It hadn't been enough. Not enough time with her. I needed more. So much more. I said a silent prayer to God that he'd give it to me. To us.

Edge got out after pulling up and stopping behind another SUV that was parked in front of Maeve's house. When a man got out, I recognized him.

"Hey, Jagger. Long time no see." We shook hands.

"You guys heading inside? You want me to wait out here?"

"Actually, another set of eyes would be welcome." When I was at the house earlier, I confirmed Maeve wasn't, looked for any sign of struggle, but that was it. A more thorough search was definitely in order. At the very least, it would kill time until Steel could get his hands on security footage from the businesses along South Congress.

I mainly watched once we went inside. Jagger and Edge took their time, searching for clues to Maeve's disappearance, but didn't come up with any more than I had—which was nothing.

"It's either dumb luck, or whoever parked that truck knows the businesses on South Congress better than I do. There's nothing," reported Steel a few hours after Edge and I were on our way to my ranch, not knowing anything more about Maeve's whereabouts now than we had before.

Saying he wanted to go home to check on Rebel, Edge dropped me off, turned around, and left. When I walked inside, Money, Decker, and Fury were seated at one of the folding tables, all three on computers.

There was no point in updating them. Steel already had about nothing turning up on the security footage, and we'd turned up nothing at Maeve's house.

"Hammer," said Money, standing to greet me.

"I'm not sure what to say other than I'm sorry," I said when he approached and shook my hand.

"My sister is an adult. At least legally. As I told you, I don't profess to understand her actions. I never have."

There were several questions I wanted to ask, including why he'd had no idea her family owned Mary Donoghue's, but now wasn't the time. I also didn't care for his barb about her being an adult.

However, my irritation was likely related more to my lack of sleep. As hard as it was to admit, if I didn't get some rest soon, I would be of no use to Maeve or anyone looking for her.

"I'll be upstairs if you need me for anything." My eyes met Decker's, and he nodded. I turned to Money. "You and I need to chat."

He followed me up the stairs. I led him to an empty bedroom and closed the door.

"I know why Maeve came to Texas."

"Start talking."

After I'd told Money everything I knew and he went downstairs, I must've drifted off because when I heard Fury saying my name and looked at my watch, it was four hours later.

"We have a development," she said, motioning for me to follow her downstairs.

"What's going on?" I asked when I saw Money hovering near Decker's computer while he talked to someone on the phone.

"Hang on, Hammer's here. I'll put you on speaker," Deck told whoever he was talking to.

"Hey, Hammer, Money," said Edge.

"Repeat what you just told me."

"I took Rebel to the Branch and was helping her, Darrow, and Quint get situated for the day when in walks McGregor."

It sounded as though Edge was in a vehicle, so I hovered over Deck's computer like Money was and watched as the app he had pulled up tracked Edge's location.

"Who's with you?"

"No one. Ink and Rage are in another vehicle, also tailing this arsehole."

"Did he say anything when he came in?"

"Affirmative. He cornered Bunker, since Tres has Sundays off, and asked about any recent visits from the ABT. Flashed him a wad of cash to help him make contact."

"What did Bunker do?"

"Took the money and said he'd do what he could. McGregor gave him a phone number to call."

Something was wrong with this picture. The ABT and the Westies were allies. Why would the latter's number two need anyone's help making contact?

"Burner phone," said Decker, confirming what I'd already suspected.

I studied the map on the screen. Edge was headed to the southeast part of Austin, an area that was primarily industrial.

"What kind of backup have you got?" I asked.

"Steel, Shredder, and Jagger are already in Austin, watching our progress and getting close."

"Any sign he suspects he's being tailed?"

"I'm pretty fucking good at this, Hammer," said Edge, chuckling.

"Answer the question."

"He doesn't have a damn clue."

"How do you want to handle this?" I asked, looking between Decker and Money.

"You go, and take Rip with you. I'll stay here and monitor activity. If you feel like you need more backup, let me know," said Deck. "Put me on the vehicle's speakerphone, and I'll give you the play-by-play."

"I'll go with you," said Money, closing his laptop and sticking it under his arm.

We'd be late to the party, so to speak, but there was no way I could stay here, wondering if Maeve was wherever McGregor was headed. I knew Money couldn't stand around here, either.

I opened the back passenger door of Rip's SUV, but Money motioned me to the front, then glanced at his computer.

"Copy that," I said, even though he hadn't spoken. He was about to log into some part of the agency's network, not something he wanted me to be able to see if I were seated behind him.

We were a few minutes into the drive when I heard Decker chuckle. "Fuck, this was too easy. Which means they're either idiots or something's up."

22

Maeve

"You've got my attention. Start talking."

I shook my head. I didn't want Tweedledum and Tweedledee listening in on our conversation. They'd left the room, but I didn't know how far they'd gone or even how big this apartment was. The loo I'd used was just off the living room.

"As I said, I'll talk to you and only you."

He nodded, perhaps in understanding, and stood.

"You could untie me," I said when he came back after ushering the two goons out.

"Or not." He pulled up the same chair he'd sat in earlier, just as close.

"Let's hear it, Mary Maeve Donoghue McTiernan."

"You know my full name. I don't even know your first."

"You don't need to know my name."

"Not very friendly of you."

"I have no interest in being your friend. Start talking, or we're finished here."

"Since you know who I am, you know what I'm worth."

"You're about to offer me money?" He looked around the apartment and laughed. "I don't need your money, Dublin."

My eyes scrunched, and I studied him. "Why did you call me that?"

"Isn't that what your *friends* call you?"

"You don't look familiar, and neither do your henchman. Who have you had following me?"

He leaned forward, and his evil eyes bored into mine. "Talk. Now," he bellowed.

"Gallagher has something that belongs to me. I want it back. What happens to him after that is none of my concern."

"If it were as easy as that to draw him out, we wouldn't have needed you."

"Whoever got your intel has misled you. The man you want is hiding from me as much as he must be from you."

"What's your offer?"

"His colleague is looking for me. We let him find me, and you'll be lying in wait."

As he studied me, I wondered if that would be enough. If not, we'd be sitting in this apartment for a *feckin'* long time if he still believed "Cormac" would come for me.

"Why would his 'colleague' be looking for you if Gallagher is hiding from you?"

"I would think that's obvious."

"Enlighten me."

"To kill me before I kill him."

The man nodded.

"Why are you looking for him? You said he took something precious from you. What?"

He stood and walked over to the window like he had earlier. "Not what. Who."

23

Hammer

"Go in slow," we heard Decker say to Edge over the SUV's speaker. "It could be a trap."

"Roger that," he said. "Switching to the comm. I'm headed in. Ink and Rage will go in with me. Steel, Shredder, and Jagger are all in position."

I couldn't help but notice Edge didn't give Decker a smart-ass response, although he was damned good at extractions too. Better than he was at tailing someone.

We remained silent, all three of us studying the screen on the dashboard even though there was no visual.

"McGregor's in, and we're right behind him."

We continued listening as our team ordered the two men to stand down and drop their weapons. I could hear Ink announcing the all clear on hidden areas.

"We got McGregor and Gallagher. All rooms cleared. No sign of Maeve."

"Fuck," I mumbled under my breath. Like Decker said, it had been too easy. Either they were holding her elsewhere, or someone else had her. I intended to utilize any means possible to figure out which.

When we arrived at the industrial complex and found the unit where the team held the two Westies, the first thing I saw was Steel positioned near a door. Edge had reported Shredder was also in position, but as intended, I didn't see him.

We parked, and Rip and I readied our weapons before getting out. "What do you want to do?" I asked Money.

"Let me know when you want me to join you inside."

"Roger that."

We were greeted by Jagger, who motioned us through the door. Ink and Rage were already working over the two assholes, who were tied to chairs. I wished I'd been there to see Gallagher's reaction when they approached McGregor and him. Scared shitless, I'd bet.

I pulled out my stogie and stood far enough off to the side that I wouldn't interfere with the boys' "prep work" but close enough that my presence was commanding.

When Ink stepped away to wipe his hands and face, I walked closer. Rage also took a step back.

"Where is she?"

"I don't know what the fuck you're talking about," rasped Gallagher through the blood and spit in his mouth.

I motioned to Ink, who gave him another pop in his already broken nose.

"Try again. Where is Maeve?"

"How the fuck would I know?"

I motioned to Ink to proceed, but before he could administer any more pain, Gallagher raised his head.

"Last time I saw her was in Ireland."

"How about you?" I asked, turning to McGregor and motioning to Rage. Evidently, this guy had a lower threshold for pain because, after a couple more hits, he passed out.

"Sir?" said Rage. I didn't know what he was asking, but I nodded anyway. He disappeared, but came back with two sledgehammers. I appreciated the irony. He handed one to Ink, and they both waited.

"Why are you trying to set up a meeting with the ABT?" I asked McGregor when he came to.

"He was." He did a slight head nod toward Gallagher, probably hurting too much to move it more than that.

Ink took a step toward Gallagher, rolled his shoulders, and swung the hammer into the concrete floor, like he was getting warmed up.

"Why?" I demanded.

When he shook his head, I turned to Ink. "He's useless. Give me a minute, and you can finish him off."

"No!" Gallagher screamed as best he could, considering the state of his face.

"How about you?" I asked the other one. "You done talking?"

When I nodded to Rage, he swung in the direction of the guy's kneecap.

"The ABT has her," he shouted seconds before impact. Rage pulled the swing outward and to the right, missing the man's leg.

"Keep talking."

"They have her, and they want Gallagher in exchange."

"Why?"

"They want him dead."

I grabbed another chair and pulled it up in front of Gallagher.

"Why would you ask for a meeting with someone who wants to kill you? Death wish? If that's the case, we're happy to oblige."

When he didn't respond, I stood and Ink stepped forward, swinging his arm that held the hammer. Rage did the same thing, only walking toward McGregor.

"Who's gonna talk first, I wonder."

McGregor didn't disappoint. "He has something he wants to exchange for his life."

I rubbed my hands together. "Now we're getting somewhere. Lemme guess. You stole something while you were in Ireland."

Gallagher's eyes met mine.

"In that case, I'll make the deal instead. Give me what you took, and *I* won't kill you."

"I'm still a dead man."

"Pretty much." I turned to the other guy. "How about you? Is there a price on your head too?"

"I'm just the middleman."

I walked over to him. "Then, you're in a better position to negotiate than he is."

"What do you want?"

"It all. I want you to get Maeve's whereabouts *and* what your buddy stole. In exchange, you can tell the ABT we'll hand him over."

"No fucking way!" shouted Gallagher. "You're gonna let them kill me?"

Ink grabbed his face and squeezed hard. "Shut your fucking mouth and listen, asshole."

"You play along, and you and your pal here get to live. You don't, well, then you don't."

"You're gonna keep me alive?" said Gallagher. "Against the ABT? No way."

I nodded at Rip, who went out of the door we came in. A couple of minutes later, he returned with Money.

"Gentlemen, I'd like to introduce Kellen McTiernan. I'm sure the last name, at least, rings a bell. If not, the most important thing you should know is Kellen is Maeve's older brother. He's also the director of the Central Intelligence Agency."

Neither man could open their eyes very wide, given they were nearly swollen closed.

"Which of you fuckwads stole from my sister?" Money asked, stepping closer. Based on the look of confusion on Edge's face, McTiernan hadn't told anyone what I told him about why his sister came to Texas.

I had to admit, I'd never considered Money much of a physical threat. The man was the word "nerd" personified. However, in this instance, the anger with which he spoke would've scared even me.

"That one," I answered, pointing to Gallagher.

Money nodded to Ink, who slammed his fist in the guy's face.

"Anything else you want me to do to him, boss?" Ink asked, swinging the sledgehammer.

"Not yet." He got in Gallagher's face. *"Where is it?"*

"Safe-deposit box."

"That's unfortunate. We can't very well take you in, looking like this. Edge, we'll need to get a warrant."

"Yes, sir."

"What bank?"

Gallagher hesitated long enough that McTiernan nodded a second time. Ink smiled, swung the sledgehammer, and took out his kneecap. The man let out a bloodcurdling scream.

Money turned to McGregor. "Your turn. What bank?"

"Bank of Texas on Ben White Street."

"Get that fucking warrant," Money barked.

"On it, sir," said Edge, pulling out his phone.

"You ready to talk yet?"

Gallagher—barely conscious—nodded.

"Who's the box registered to?"

"Cormac Moran," he grunted.

He turned to McGregor. "Where's my sister?"

"I don't know."

"Where's my fucking sister?" McTiernan got in his face, and Rage stepped forward.

"All I know is the ABT has her."

"You better pray she's still alive, or I'll make every one of your fucking nightmares a reality." Money pulled out his phone and appeared to be sending a text. "Who's your contact?"

"Stillman Robinson."

Robinson? What the fuck. I looked over at Edge, whose head snapped up. He took several steps forward.

"Repeat that."

McGregor said the name a second time, and Edge's eyes met mine.

"Who called the hit on you?" I asked Gallagher.

He hesitated for a split second until Ink lifted the hammer.

"Robinson did."

"Why?"

"I'll answer that," said Edge. "You killed his brother."

Gallagher nodded.

Robinson. I knew the name sounded familiar. First name Thomas, aka Possum. Edge's gut had been dead on.

Money was looking at something on his phone. "You said the ABT had Maeve."

McGregor nodded.

"Stillman Robinson is with the Nazi Freedom Riders."

"They merged," said Rip. "Robinson moved into the number one position with the ABT."

I walked closer to Edge. "Who've you got inside?"

"Vex."

I knew the name but had never worked with the guy. "I don't care what you have to do. Find him and find out where the fuck they're holding Maeve."

If he couldn't get his hands on Gallagher, Stillman Robinson would avenge his brother's death on anyone he could.

I spun around when a phone rang.

"It's him or someone who works for him," said McGregor, nodding his head in the direction of his jacket.

"Have you spoken to him already?"

"No, but he's the only person with that number."

I grabbed the phone. "McGregor," I answered.

"You have something I want," the voice seethed.

"You have something I want. Let's trade."

24

Maeve

The man got up and walked out the door of the apartment. Ten minutes later, he returned and stood looking out the window.

"Well?" I demanded. "What happens now?"

"We wait."

"Are you going to kill me?"

"What makes you ask?"

"You kidnapped me. I can identify you."

"Thank you for pointing that out."

"What Gallagher has of mine may seem valuable, but it isn't."

"And?"

"It wouldn't be worth killing me for."

"As long as I get Gallagher, I don't care."

"What did he do?"

The man was silent long enough that I knew he had no intention of answering me. After several more minutes of dead air, there was a knock at the door.

He walked over, opened it, and took a bag from one of his goons.

"What is that?"

"Food."

"I'm not hungry."

"I didn't say it was for you."

He went into the kitchen, and as he opened the various containers, my stomach growled in anticipation after I inhaled aromas I was so familiar with.

"Is this the part where you torture me?"

He came out with two plates heaped with Billy and Alicia's specialties. After setting them on the table behind me, he untied the ropes that kept me bound to the chair, then untied my hands.

"You're very trusting," I said, picking up the knife and fork sitting beside the plate.

He proceeded to eat—and continued to ignore me.

25

Hammer

Edge, Rip, and I crafted the plan for how the exchange would go down. While Robinson had agreed to come alone, I didn't believe he would any more than he thought I would. Not that it would be me facilitating the handoff. Rip would be.

McGregor swore on his life that he'd never met Stillman or anyone with the ABT, and if the organization had somehow gotten the same photos of the man Decker had, Rip looked enough like him to get away with it. Not that the real man looked anything like himself presently.

Robinson had also agreed to my request to do the exchange tonight at twenty-hundred hours at the historic First Pentecostal Church on Sixth and Hancock.

Edge thought it best to send Rip, Steel, and Shredder to get set up at the church early, and I concurred. The team tonight would consist of more than that, but they could determine placement now.

As much as I wanted to be the first to lay eyes on Maeve, I was sure Money felt the same way.

"Tres is on his way with a package for you, boys," Deck said through the comm. "Got some new toys I want you to try out."

"Copy that," I responded at the same time Edge did.

When it came to "spy toys," Ashford was a fucking genius. Only one other man in the world could claim to be on par with him, and that man had been Deck's mentor. While I didn't usually participate in any of the Invincibles' missions, that had changed recently when we had to do an extraction from a tiger preserve in India. Without the use of Decker's spyware, I doubted any of us would have made it out alive.

I wondered what Money was studying on his computer and what he believed Maeve would do once her extraction was successful. As far as I could tell, he had no authority over any decisions she made or her wealth.

There was still the matter of the community service she'd need to complete to satisfy the charges against her. I doubted Ringer would let those slide even though she'd been kidnapped. More, I wasn't sure the details would ever be made public.

The plan we'd collectively agreed to, on our side of the op, was to rescue Maeve but to stop short of handing Gallagher over to Robinson or anyone else from the ABT. Instead, the man would be arrested and stand trial for murder, grand theft, and whatever else went along with those.

As far as Maeve's kidnapping, it wouldn't be easy for Money to look the other way and let those responsible escape charges. Robinson in particular, but McTiernan hadn't brought it up, so we didn't either.

When Tres arrived, he handed the package off to me and left.

I called Decker, who ran us through the use of technology only previously seen in movies. Hard to say which came first in this case. If I were a betting man, I'd lay all my money on Ashford being the one who'd originally thought of it, rather than a Hollywood screenwriter.

The devices allowed for audio and video recording through a smart contact lens that went in one eye only.

Each of us outfitted could also view live action. That, along with starting and ending the recording, was controlled by a blink pattern, as were the zoom and volume. The most surprising thing to me was how the lens I put in didn't feel any differently than the contacts I wore before I had surgery to correct my vision.

Utilizing this technology, each of us would be able to see what was happening in real time. It wouldn't be limited to Rip's view either. Anyone, including those surveilling the scene, could transmit what they saw to Decker, who would then alert us through the comm system. Thus, an adversary's ambush would be nearly impossible to carry out.

The other, more common technology we'd be making use of was a Doppler radar to determine the number of people in the immediate vicinity and where they were in relation to the exchange location.

The closer the clock got to our planned departure, the more anxious I became. This wasn't just a mission to carry out; this was personal. My sole desired outcome was Maeve's safe rescue. Any other objectives were inconsequential to me. Maybe that's how Money felt too.

"Got it," said Money, closing his laptop and motioning me over. He'd been waiting for the warrant that would allow us access to Gallagher's safe-deposit box.

Not receiving it before the end of the business day may have been cause to delay the exchange, something no one wanted to address.

Edge tossed me the keys to his SUV. The bank was less than fifteen minutes from our current location, but the drive there seemed endless.

"Any idea what we'll find?" I asked him.

Money shook his head. "I was going to ask you the same thing."

"Whatever it is, it's priceless to your sister." I stuck my stogie in the pocket humidor and rubbed the top of my head. "Can I ask you something?"

Money grinned but didn't bother giving me the pat answer we always used. "You can ask."

"How come you never looked into Maeve's family's background?"

"Why would you think I haven't?"

"You never said a word about it. Given their ownership of Mary Donoghue's, I would've thought you'd mention it in our initial conversation."

"It wasn't relevant. Regardless of any experience she did or didn't have, purchasing the Long Branch was—is—a mistake. Admittedly, I hope she changes her mind about doing so as a result of this ordeal."

Or she'd need to consider private security, given her vast wealth. After seeing how happy she'd been the first night we worked the bar together, I wondered if Money still would've discouraged her had he witnessed it.

When we arrived at the bank and went inside, we were approached by a woman. After Money explained our reason for being there, she led us to the branch manager's office.

"I'll need to see the warrant and some ID," the man said once Money repeated what he'd told the woman. While I'm sure I would've been impatient, Money calmly removed both from his pocket, handed the warrant over, and showed him his ID. The man looked from it to Money and back again.

Without a word, he typed something into his computer and sat back in his chair. His eyes widened, and he stood, presumably when whatever he was looking for confirmed Money's identity.

"Right this way, sir," the man said, not even questioning who I was or why I was there. I suppose my being with the director of the Central Intelligence Agency was credential enough.

"I'll wait here," I volunteered when the man opened the vault.

McTiernan shook his head and motioned for me to follow. The manager used two keys to unlock the box, pulled it from the slot, and handed it over.

"Would you like a privacy room?" he asked.

Money said we would, and we were led out of the vault.

When he slid the lid open, a single item lay at the bottom. "What is it?" I asked.

"I believe it's the Tara Brooch."

"The Tara what?"

"It's a Celtic brooch circa 750 AD. It was reported to be 'discovered' in the mid-eighteen hundreds, but I'd heard rumors that it wasn't verified as the real brooch."

"Why would Maeve have it?" I wondered out loud.

Money smiled. "When it comes to the Marys, nothing surprises me."

"Your awareness of them would surprise your sister."

Money nodded. "We've never been particularly close."

"Yet you've made it your business to know hers."

"It's the promise I made to our father."

"I know I'm way out of line with what I'm about to say, but I believe it would make her happy to know that."

"Or piss her off for not respecting her privacy."

Money's gaze met mine. "We need to make sure she comes out of this unscathed. I cannot accept any other outcome."

I felt the same way.

26

Maeve

"It's time to go," said the man who'd left me untied the rest of the day, although not unattended.

"Where are you takin' me?"

"To church. Turn around."

"Oh, for God's sake," I grumbled when he tied my hands behind my back and blindfolded me. "This isn't necessary. You're about to let me go anyway."

"I'm not letting you go. I'm trading you."

"You were also to ensure I get back what Gallagher stole from me."

I couldn't see him because he'd covered my eyes, but his lack of response concerned me.

"Did you hear me?"

"I heard you."

"I want what's mine. It was part of our deal."

He led me out of the apartment and into an elevator.

"I can't *feckin'* believe this," I said under my breath, willing myself not to cry. I'd not get my brooch returned to me; that much was becoming obvious.

Something my mother and her mother had entrusted to me was now in the hands of the worst kind of man, one I guessed would be dead before midnight.

"You're not getting your 'precious person' back, so I'm not getting what I wanted either, is that it? I've already told you it's not as valuable as you think. At least monetarily."

"Stop. Talking."

"Start talking. Stop talking," I muttered. "You're a *feckin' eejit*."

"And you're a pain in the ass."

The drive we took from where they'd held me to wherever they were "trading" me was a series of right turns. One after the other. There was no sense in trying to confuse me, given I well recognized the apartment building and knew its location. All the driver was doing was making me nauseated. It would serve the bastard right if I lost the contents of my stomach all over his vehicle.

The car came to a stop, the door opened beside me, and the same man I'd spent a silent afternoon with hauled me out of the backseat. If I hadn't recognized the feel of his hand on my arm, I would've recognized his cologne. Not that he overdid it. If the man wasn't the devil incarnate, I might've found him attractive. Instead, the image I couldn't wipe from my mind was of Hammer, naked and standing before me. Would any man ever measure up to him?

Here I was, about to be exchanged for the man I hated with every breath I took, and I was thinking about sex. There was something seriously wrong with the way my brain worked. Or maybe it was just a coping mechanism. If I allowed myself to overthink what was about to happen, the fear might be debilitating.

I was led up steps and waited as I listened to a heavy door creak open. "Wait."

"What?" the man snapped.

"If you don't intend to honor the deal you made with me, at least let me look at the man one more time. Let me see the fear in his eyes. I beg you." I wasn't certain this man intended to kill Gallagher, but it seemed likely.

He didn't let go of my arm, so someone else must've untied the blindfold. It took a minute for my eyes to adjust to the low light of what was—as he'd said—a church.

"I don't see anyone."

"They're here."

We walked up the aisle and stood before the steps of the altar. Moments later, Rip appeared in a doorway. In that instant, I saw something in his eyes. I looked up at my captor, and it was almost as if they recognized each other. What in the bloody hell was happening here? Who was Rip, truly?

Every thought of anything flew from my brain when I saw him practically dragging the man I'd known as Cormac Moran out into the open. He'd been beaten to a bloody pulp, and something was wrong with one of his legs. If my captor didn't intend to kill him, he looked like he might die anyway.

I screamed when I was suddenly pushed to the floor amidst the sound of men shouting at someone to drop their weapons, followed immediately by gunfire.

The man who I thought intended to kill me earlier covered my body with his own until the gunshots ceased. "Stay down," he said, easing himself from on top of me.

27

Hammer

"Well, I'll be damned. No wonder the fucker didn't make contact," I heard Decker say through my earpiece shortly after I watched the two men who'd come in with Robinson be shot and killed after being warned by Edge and Ink to drop their weapons.

"What the hell?" I muttered as I ran inside in time to see Stillman, who'd covered Maeve's body with his own, gingerly move away from her, then help her up.

"How the hell are you?" said Edge, rushing forward to hug the guy who was the head of an organization he detested.

"Who in the fuck is that?" I said into the comm.

"Vex! The asshole," answered Decker.

"Vex?" The one undercover with the ABT? He couldn't have let any of us know she was safe?

I heard the sound of sirens getting closer to our location, presumably because of the gunshots fired.

"Did you know about this?" I barked at Decker.

"You'll want to take back that question, Hammer. We have known each other a damn long time, and if you think I'd keep this from you—"

"Sorry," I muttered, watching Maeve and her brother embrace. God, how I wished I could do the same.

"Where's the real Stillman Robinson?" I asked.

"In custody, awaiting trial," responded Money, backing away from his sister.

Before I could lose my temper on him, the doors of the church flew open. I turned around and raised my hands in the air. The last person I expected to see in front of the pack of law enforcement was Mac.

"I called in a special favor from Austin PD to be able to be here for this. Wish I could've gotten them to let me bring Rebel along. She deserves to see this miserable life-form carted off." He motioned to where Rip stood beside Gallagher.

I was seconds away from going ballistic on everyone in this church, demanding to know who knew what and when, when I felt a hand on my back.

"Hammer?"

I turned to face her, and Maeve fell into my embrace. She put her arms around my neck and held on to me as tightly as I was her. "Thank God you're safe," I whispered.

"It appears I was safer than I realized."

I leaned back and looked into her eyes. "I was as in the dark as you were, Dublin."

Two men with a stretcher walked past us, presumably for Gallagher, who looked ready to pass out, if he hadn't already.

"This is gonna be one hell of a hotwash," said Decker, chuckling. "Signing off and heading home. You know how to reach me *tomorrow*."

I took the earpiece out and stuck it in my pocket.

"Wait!" Maeve shouted as the stretcher carrying Gallagher was about to pass us by. "He's got—"

"This?" I asked, pulling the brooch from my other pocket, where I'd had it wrapped in a handkerchief.

"What in the bloody hell? How? You know what? I don't give a *feck*." She put her arms around my neck, pulled until I leaned down, and we kissed.

"I was unaware Vex was undercover as Robinson," said Money, approaching Maeve and me. "Until Decker identified him, I had no idea who had you."

"He's one of you, then? That explains a lot."

"Such as?" I asked.

"Let's get out of here," Edge said before Maeve could answer. "I can't wait to tell Rebel that the man who killed Possum is *finally* in custody. Ink and Rage will deal with Mac and Austin PD to get this wrapped up."

"How did Mac know this was going down?" I asked.

"He said it was an anonymous tip."

From whom, I wondered. Decker?

"You're a good actor," Maeve said when Vex approached.

"Had to be. Both our lives depended on it."

"I'm Sterling Anderson," I reached out to shake the man's hand.

"Nice to finally meet you, Hammer. Bronson Dunning, or Vex as most call me."

"Ready?" asked Edge, motioning with his head.

Maeve clung to my arm on our way past the two dead men who lay in the aisle.

"Best not to look. Keep your eyes on me."

She nodded.

"Would you like us to drop you and Money at your place?" I asked once we were in the SUV and pulling away from the church.

"Oh. Um. I suppose. If I'm no longer in your custody."

"You were never in my custody, but if you'd rather stay at the ranch—"

"*Yes.*" She leaned into me. "I don't think my brother would be keen on me climbing into bed beside him when nightmares plague me."

I smiled. "Probably not."

"You, on the other hand."

"Yes, I, on the other hand, wouldn't *allow* you to sleep anywhere other than next to me."

I could see Money's profile from where I sat in the backseat with his sister and wondered what he must be thinking. Not that I'd attempt to hide the fact that we were more than client and attorney now. The conversation would need to take place, though.

"I should give Fury a call and let her know we're on our way."

Maeve pulled away, folded her arms, and looked out the opposite window. I put the phone down.

"Is there a problem?"

"We'll discuss it later," she snapped.

"She's your new attorney. You need to tell me right now if that's going to be an issue." While I'd lowered my voice, I was sure Money and Edge could hear us.

"I can't believe the *only* attorney you could find to take your place was one you've slept with." Whispering did nothing to hide the fact that she was pissed.

"Slept with? What are you talking about?"

"*Shush!* Lower your voice. I was there when she reminded you she'd already spent at least one night in your bed."

"Oh!" I shook my head and tried not to laugh. "What you heard was her reminding me of the night I walked in on *her and Rip* in my bed."

"What?"

"I arrived ahead of schedule, and while I'd messaged Fury to let her know I'd be there within the hour, as soon as I walked in, I realized she must not have seen it."

She studied me.

"I told you once or twice you'd know if I lied to you."

"Her and Rip?"

I nodded.

"Interesting. I have to tell you, for a minute, I thought he was a bad guy."

"Rip? Why?"

"I saw a look pass between Vex and him." Maeve opened her palm, and I saw she had the brooch clasped in it. "Thank you for returning this to me."

"Actually, you should thank your brother."

Maeve unfastened her seat belt, practically crawled over the seat, and kissed Money's cheek. "Thank you, Kellen."

He smiled. "You're welcome, Mary Maeve Donoghue McTiernan."

She plopped down beside me and refastened her seat belt. "You told him."

"He already knew. He also knew what that was." I pointed to the brooch.

"They trusted me to keep it safe. I almost didn't."

"The Marys?"

She beamed. "Yes, the Marys."

I leaned into her so my mouth was next to her ear. "Your father trusted your brother to keep you safe."

"And I almost didn't," said Money.

"Well, we both did in the end, so that's that." Maeve made a motion like she was brushing off her hands.

Edge dropped Maeve, Money, and me at the ranch. "I'll see you tomorrow for the hotwash."

"It doesn't look like anyone is here," I said, opening the front door and motioning Maeve and her brother inside.

My brow furrowed in confusion when she made a beeline for the kitchen.

"I don't know about the two of you, but I could use a shot or two of this." She held up an unopened bottle of bourbon I didn't know I had. "Compliments of Mr. Ashford," she said, holding up a note.

"I'll get the glasses."

Maeve motioned Money to follow and led him into the kitchen and over to the table.

"Your sister helped me move some things around," I said, setting the glasses in front of her. "I'm not very good at the whole decorating thing."

I winked and she smiled. Money, on the other hand, didn't.

"I guess now's as good a time as any for us to have this conversation."

 He looked from me to Maeve.

"Yes, Kellen, Hammer and I had sex, and we plan to have more. Before you pop a filling, he's no longer my attorney. Someone named *Fury* is."

"I'm glad to hear she passed the bar."

"You know her, then?"

"Ellison used to work for me."

Maeve raised a brow.

"If I remember correctly, you're the one who gave her the code name."

"She had quite the temper." Money nodded and raised a brow at his sister. "Much like someone else I know."

She smacked him, then nudged me. "Hammer calls me Dublin, and I call him Drip."

The man I'd rarely seen laugh, did. "Drip. Hmm."

"No."

He laughed again. "Not willing to make a permanent change, eh?"

"Not even a temporary one."

After two more shots each, we called it a night, parting ways when we got to the top of the stairs.

"That went better than I expected," I confessed once we'd closed the bedroom door behind us.

"You're a far better cry than most of the blokes I've been with."

"Gee, thanks."

Maeve put her arms around my waist. "You know I've always gone for the bad guys, right? It makes sense now why I wasn't attracted to Vex."

"Because he wasn't really a bad guy?"

"Yes, but I kept comparing him to you."

"He's a lot younger. Closer to your age."

"Age doesn't matter to me. It shouldn't matter to you either." As she said the words, she unfastened my belt. "I need you naked, Hammer. Imagining you that way is the only thing that got me through. And before you say it, yes, I know I'm weird."

"Just naked? No red hero cape as I flew in to rescue you?"

Maeve put her hands on my chest and looked into my eyes. "I knew you would."

"It wasn't just me."

"I don't care about the others. Except Kellen, of course. I was surprised you allowed him to enter the state."

"I couldn't have kept him away if I wanted to, and I didn't. He really cares about you, Maeve."

"Aye, I know he does. But…"

"What?"

"Can we please stop talking about Kellen now?"

It might make me sound like the old man I was, but Maeve and I didn't have sex; we made love until we both fell into a sound sleep.

Sometime in the middle of the night, I woke from what I thought was the best dream I'd ever had, only to open my eyes and see Maeve stroking my cock.

"Good, you're awake," she said, pushing me to my back, then straddling me and guiding me into her hot, wet pussy. I let her set her own rhythm, reached between us, and swirled my finger around her clit.

When her body shuddered in release, I rolled us so she was beneath me.

"Look at me," I said. "Keep your eyes on me."

This time, I set our pace, alternating between hard and fast, then deep and slow. Maeve's eyes stayed focused on mine. When she put her hand on my tattoo and sunk her nails into my skin, I let myself go, knowing she'd come along with me. I drew her up into my arms and kissed her; even then she didn't close her eyes, and neither did I.

28

Maeve

I waited for Hammer to realize, like I had, that we'd both been so swept up in the moment that we'd forgotten to use a condom. Really, it was more me who'd done the sweeping.

I was on birth control, but we hadn't discussed going without protection.

"I'm sorry," I whispered.

Hammer turned to face me. "Why?"

"I forgot the condom."

"What are you worried about?"

"That you'll be unhappy with me."

He cupped my cheek with his palm and brushed my lips with his fingertips. "I'm not unhappy with you, and it isn't your responsibility alone."

"I know, but I was the…instigator."

"Are you worried about getting pregnant?"

I shook my head. "Birth control."

"It's been a long time since I've been with another woman, Maeve."

"Longer for me, I'd guess. With a man, I mean."

He smiled and yawned.

I snuggled into him. I knew, eventually, we'd have to talk about everything that had happened in the last twenty-four hours, but not tonight.

When I woke the next morning, Hammer was awake, standing by the window. He looked troubled.

"What's wrong?"

He turned to me and smiled. "Good morning, and not a thing."

I sat up. "You're lying."

Hammer walked over to the bed and sat facing me. "I really like you, Maeve."

"And I like you." Was he about to give me the brush-off? It certainly sounded like it.

"Last night, you asked if you were still 'in my custody.' You're not, and you haven't been. Initially, Mac made you staying with me a stipulation of the writ bond."

"The judge said the stipulations remain."

"I think I can get him to release them if you want to go back to your place in Austin."

I fell back against the pillow. "Does this mean buying the Long Branch is off too?"

"Too? I'm not saying anything is off. What I'm trying to tell you is that you don't have to stay here."

"Do you want me to leave?"

When he took a deep breath and let it out slowly, I braced myself. I was a big girl, or at least a grown-up. Sort of. Either way, I could handle this. I blinked away my tears, praying they wouldn't fall. God wasn't listening.

Hammer reached out and brushed one away. "Hey, now. What's this?"

"If you're dumping me, get on with it."

Instead, he pulled me into his arms, prolonging my agony.

"I'm not dumping you. If anything, I'm making it easier for you to walk away if that's what you want to do."

"Why would I want that?"

"Because I'm fourteen years older than you are. Because I live out on a ranch, and you live in the city. Because you're a free spirit who has to dance at least once a night even when you're at work."

"What have you got against dancing?"

"I love dancing, with you anyway."

"Hammer?"

"Yes?"

"If you don't want to be with me, come right out and say it. Otherwise, don't feel as though you need to think for me. I'm perfectly capable of doing that on my own. And if I decide I don't want to be with you, I'll say so."

"I don't want to hold you back—"

"Are you rethinking becoming my temporary partner at the Long Branch?"

"Yes."

I pulled back and looked into his eyes. While I was disappointed, I understood. That kind of life wasn't for everyone.

"I don't want it to be temporary."

"What are you saying?"

"I want us to buy the Branch together. I know you weren't looking for a partner, and I know you don't need the money, but I still want to."

"Let me think it over."

"Of course." Hammer shifted as if he was getting up. I grabbed his arm. "Okay. I've decided."

"And?"

"Yes. I'd like you to be my permanent partner. Now, come over here, and let's have a *cwtch*."

"I think I like these as much as dancing."

"There's just one thing. I need to return to Ireland for a bit. Not long."

"Maeve, I'm sorry to say I don't think the judge will allow it."

"Oh! Not right away. I mean I have every intention of completing whatever is required of me. It's just that we'll need to plan for it. And, Hammer, I want you to go with me. There's something very important I need to show you."

I'd lived enough of my short life keeping the Marys' secrets, not wanting anyone to know my business or even who I was, if I could prevent it. I was tired of that. Done with it, in fact.

The first step I took was when I told Hammer what had happened with Bobby. The second was revealing my background to his friends. Who already felt like my friends too. Next, I'd share the true value of the Tara Brooch—and it wasn't what anyone believed it to be.

29

Hammer

Our meeting—hotwash—was scheduled for one this afternoon, here at the *unnamed* ranch, as Mac reminded me every time he visited.

Once we finally got out of bed, Maeve and I went downstairs to find her brother sitting in the kitchen, working on his computer.

Money looked up, saw his sister, and smiled. When she walked over, put her arms around his neck, and kissed his cheek, he beamed.

I wondered if Maeve had any inkling of the rarity of either of those things.

"Anything I need to know?" I asked when Money scowled at his laptop.

"I would prefer if the ABT died a quick death. I don't even care if it's painless at this point."

Back when all the shit went down with Rebel, the Feds conducted a sting where we believed the ABT had—as Money just said—died, except news of their demise was premature. Fast forward a couple of months, and they'd returned, vowing once again to take their pound of flesh out of Rebel for Possum's death.

Now, the murderer was headed to prison for the rest of his life, whether that would be a year, ten years, or longer. I doubt many believed he'd survive incarceration for longer than a few months.

"What should I do?" Maeve asked when people began arriving.

"There will be questions about your kidnapping. After we've finished that part of the meeting, you'll be free to leave if you want." I leveled my gaze at her. "The meeting, that is."

"Can I stay?"

It really wasn't my call, but I agreed to talk it over with Money and Decker before we got started.

"Who are we waiting on?" I asked when it appeared almost everyone who had been part of the op had arrived.

"Just Mac, but I asked him to show up a little later," Deck responded.

"Mac? What about Vex?"

"He's remaining undercover," said Money. "The mission isn't over."

"That's why I asked Mac to join us. Vex has some intel we need to pass on to him," said Decker.

"Maeve asked how much of this she can sit in on."

"This is your call, not mine," Decker said, looking at Money.

"I don't have a problem with it."

"I'll let her know." I looked for her in the kitchen, but she wasn't there, so I checked upstairs and didn't see her there either. A familiar—and disconcerting—feeling came over me when something caught my eye from the bedroom window.

Maeve and Fury were seated in the Adirondack chairs by the fire pit and appeared to be in a lively conversation. The bad feeling I'd had turned to good when I saw both of them laugh.

"Sorry to interrupt, but we're ready to get started," I said once I'd gone downstairs and out the patio door.

Fury went inside first, but when Maeve went to pass, I grabbed her hand and pulled her close to me.

"I like her," she said, putting her arms around my neck when I wrapped mine around her waist.

"I like you." I brought my lips to hers and kissed her. "A lot."

"The feeling is mutual."

"You can sit in on as much of the meeting as you'd like to, but you're also free to leave if it gets to be…"

"Too gory? Never. I can't wait to hear every detail of how Cormac ended up looking like he was on death's door."

I laughed. "I was going to say boring."

"What we're going to discuss this afternoon is considered top-secret information," Money began. When he looked directly at his sister, she glared back at him. "Understood?"

"Yes, Kellen. Understood," she snapped.

"While the first objective of the mission intended to find a killer and also take down the Aryan Brotherhood of Texas organization is complete, our second objective remains. As his role wasn't compromised, Vex has resumed his undercover assignment."

Those in the room, including me, nodded.

"As Decker mentioned earlier, Sheriff MacIver will be joining us later. The reason for his attendance at this meeting is that Vex discovered one of Mac's deputies is actually an ABT mole."

"That's how he knew," murmured Maeve.

"Knew what?" I asked.

"That you called me Dublin."

Both McTiernan's and Ashford's heads shot up. "Was there a deputy who witnessed Hammer calling you that?"

"The *feckin' eejit* who escorted me from the cell."

"Did you see him too?" Deck asked me.

"Affirmative."

"Could you identify him?"

"Absolutely. I'm sure we both could."

"Good. Hammer, I'll need you and Maeve to get with Mac at some point and do just that."

"Are you saying Vex didn't know who the mole was?" I asked.

"That's right." Money's gaze fell on his sister. "Good job, Maeve. That will be of tremendous help." He cleared his throat. "Moving on, do you feel up to talking about the abduction? If not, you and I can do it later, just the two of us."

I swear to God, I almost shed a fucking tear watching and listening to the way he spoke to Maeve. I had to admit, my opinion of the guy was now far different than it had been the entire time I knew him. I wondered if others here felt the same way.

"I can do it. It wasn't…terrible. I mean, now we know why."

"Go ahead whenever you're ready."

Maeve took a deep breath and looked from her brother to me.

"I told you I was going for a walk, but once I found the key to my truck, I left the ranch instead."

"Why?" Maybe now wasn't the time for me to ask, but it was relevant.

"I, um, misunderstood something." She looked over at Fury, then returned her gaze to me. "At first, I planned to go to the Long Branch, but seeing as I was miffed, I thought it best if I cooled off a wee bit. That's why I went home."

"What happened when you got there?"

"I'd already decided to grab a few more clothes and be on my way, so I left the truck running and went inside. I should've turned around and left when I realized the alarm wasn't set, but I couldn't remember if I'd re-armed it when you and I were there the other day."

I didn't remember whether she had either, and that wasn't at all like me.

"As soon as I walked in the door, I saw a man standin' in my kitchen. Before I could turn around, another came up behind me. I kicked and screamed, but they overpowered me. One tied my hands behind my back while the other put a bag over my head."

When her voice wavered, I reached over and rubbed her back. "Take your time."

Maeve took a couple of deep breaths. "They put me in the trunk of a car. *Gawd,* my truck must be out of gas by now. I doubt those two *eejits* would've thought to turn it off."

"Someone drove it from your place and parked it on South Congress," I told her.

"My bloody phone is in it."

Edge held up an evidence bag. "It's right here. No prints but yours on it, so you can have it back." He slid it across the table.

"Maeve, did you turn your phone off intentionally?" Money asked.

"Off? Oh! No, I wouldn't have done. The battery was nearly dead, and I didn't have a charger in the truck. That was the other thing I meant to get from the house."

"Go on."

"They took me to an apartment building downtown, took the bag off my head, but tied me to a chair and left me in the dark. When morning came around and I could see more of the place, I realized I'd considered buying an apartment there." She looked at Money. "See, I followed the kidnapping-survival training protocols. *Remember as much as you can about your location.*"

He smiled. "Good job."

Good on McTiernan for having her go through something like that. It made sense, given his position along with her wealth.

"For most of the mornin', I only saw the two who'd nabbed me. They kept askin' me about Cormac, err, Gallagher, and I kept tellin' them I didn't know where the bloody bastard was or I'd have killed him myself."

"When did Vex arrive?"

"I'm not certain, but he may have been there already. I told the other two I wouldn't say another word to either of them. I got one to take me to the loo, and when I came out, the other man—Vex—was waiting."

"What happened then?"

"I tried to make a deal with him, but he wasn't so much interested in that. Then he had food delivered." Maeve looked at me. "From Billy and Alicia's." Her eyes opened wide. "He must've known we went there. Anyway, the next I knew, he said we were leaving and that he was tradin' me. I think you know most of the rest."

"Any questions up to this point?" Money asked around the table.

"I have a few," said Maeve.

Again, he smiled at her. "I'm sure you do. We'll come back around to them if that's all right with you."

"Of course."

My eyes met Decker's, and he raised a brow just like I was. *Who was this guy, and what had he done with Money?* I wanted to ask.

Once Maeve finished her recollection of what she'd seen and heard, each member of the team went through their accounting of what took place from the time she left the ranch through the aftermath of the events at the church.

Money reported the two victims were identified as John Fischer and Stephen Poltz. He said their deaths were ruled justified. He added that both Gallagher and McGregor were undergoing medical treatment at an undisclosed location and each of them would face multiple federal charges.

"While I want to state for the record that Stillman Robinson was and is in federal custody, I was not informed Mr. Dunning was undercover. Therefore, I had no idea who we were dealing with in terms of my sister's abduction."

"I gotta say, even though I wasn't there, listening to how you handled Gallagher and McGregor... McTiernan, you stepped up," said Decker.

Money laughed. "I've never had reason to unleash on any of you. However, what happened with Vex can never happen again." He looked directly at Edge. "You and I will meet offline about this."

"Yes, sir," Edge responded sheepishly.

"If we're wrapping up, I'll let the sheriff know to head in," Decker said.

Money looked around the table, but no one spoke up. "One more thing, and this has nothing to do with what I said about what happened with Vex never happening again. We're running the rest of this as an agency-driven mission. Rip will be taking the lead and will report directly to me. Any questions?"

I assumed he and Decker had already discussed this development since Ashford didn't speak up.

"Hammer? Can you spare him as necessary?"

I was about to respond when I realized Money was just giving me shit. No one knew better than I did that the mission came first.

When everyone got up to stretch their legs, Maeve leaned over to me.

"I can't believe I'm saying this, but I am getting a little bored."

I chuckled. "Me too, to be honest. I'll see if we can skip Mac's part of the meeting."

"I don't want to steal you away."

"I can't tell you how much I wish you would."

"I was thinking of taking a nap."

"I'll join you as long as we can have…What's it called again?"

"A *cwtch*?"

"Yeah. That. A bunch of them."

30

Maeve

We hadn't been in bed long before Hammer was fast asleep. Rather than drift off myself, I studied him.

What was it about this man that had me knocking my walls down? I never dreamed I'd tell a soul the secret of the Tara Brooch. In fact, I wondered what might happen if it went with me to my grave.

Now, I wasn't thinking of only telling him. I also planned to tell Kellen.

After lying awake for nearly an hour, I eased off the bed so as not to wake Hammer and crept downstairs. I didn't see anyone in the room where the meeting had taken place, so I went looking in the kitchen.

"Hey, you. I thought you were napping," my brother said when I walked in.

"Couldn't sleep."

"Come and sit."

"Am I interrupting?"

"Not at all. I'm making arrangements to return to DC."

"There's something I want to discuss with you."

"If it's about the Long Branch, my opinion hasn't changed, but if you still want to buy it, I'll stop being a fuddy-duddy about it."

I covered my mouth to stifle my laugh. "Fuddy-duddy? You sound like Da. Or even Granny, although you never met my mum's mum."

"What was she like?"

"I'm a lot like her, or so those who knew her say."

"My guess is all the Marys have been independent, free-spirited dynamos."

I raised a brow. "Thank you, Kellen."

He reached out and took my hand. "I hate that it took almost losing you for me to realize I've never told you how much you mean to me or how much I respect you. When Da, as you call him, asked me to look out for you, I took the 'parental figure' thing too far."

"I'm sure I needed it."

"So. You and Hammer?"

"It's a thing, Kellen."

"Yeah? Should I tell you I approve, or would it be best if you believe I don't?"

I swatted him. "I want you to tell me the truth."

"I have great respect for everyone who was in the meeting earlier, along with the rest of their team, including Hammer. Maybe him most of all."

"Why most of all?"

"Do you know he was a Marine Ranger? That probably doesn't mean anything to you, but I can tell you, they are badass."

"First fuddy-duddy, now badass. I don't know what to make of you, brother."

"Me neither, to tell you the truth. But back to Hammer. There was a mission recently. It was more MI6 than CIA, but the man who led it is a good friend of Hammer's and mine. In fact, we were just in London for the man's wedding. The mission was dangerous, I can tell you that much, and your 'boyfriend' volunteered. What's more, I doubt he would've taken no for an answer. Not that anyone would've tried to talk him out of it. He's also a damned good attorney."

"He's a good man."

"The best."

"I know I haven't always made the best decisions, but Hammer and I are talking about partnering in the bar. Buying it together, I mean."

"Not that you're asking for my approval, but I'm giving it anyway."

"I have a few legal *issues* to take care of, but Hammer thinks we can proceed with the purchase contract, and by the time it goes through, I should have it all dealt with."

"I'm glad to hear it, Maeve."

"So, once I've completed the judge's requirements, I need to go back to Ireland to take care of something. I've already asked Hammer to go with me, but I'd like you to go too."

"I'm intrigued. What's this about?"

"It relates to the Tara Brooch."

"Now I'm even more intrigued."

"Yeah, well, don't try using your spy friends to figure it out. They won't be able to."

"Let me know when you want to go, and I'll be honored to go along."

"I think I'll go join Hammer and try to sleep a bit. When are you leaving?"

"I haven't figured that out yet."

"Can you stay a couple more days? I'd like to take you to the Branch at least once."

"I can do that."

When I eased the door to the bedroom open, I saw Hammer was awake. "Sorry, I tried not to disturb you."

He held out his hand, and I got in bed beside him. "Couldn't sleep?"

"Not so much. I talked to Kellen."

"Yeah?"

"I asked him to go to Ireland with us. I also told him I wanted to take him to the Branch."

"What did he say?"

"Yes to both, astonishingly."

"He loves you."

"Aye. I love him too."

I looked into Hammer's kind eyes. There was so much more I wanted to say, but I didn't know where to begin. "Thank you for all you've done for me," I finally said.

He stroked my cheek. "You're welcome."

"You're a good man, Drip."

"That means a lot coming from you, Dublin."

Once again, the Long Branch was packed by the time Hammer and I arrived with Kellen.

"Do what you need to do," he said when I hesitated before sitting beside him at the bar.

I raised a brow, and he laughed.

"I want to see you in your element."

"Come on then, Drip. We've work to do."

My brother laughed again. I couldn't remember seeing him do much of that when I was growing up. Mainly, he was broody and so bloody smart he intimidated the hell out of me.

"What are you thinking about?" Hammer asked, perhaps noticing my furrowed brow.

"My brother seems…different."

He surprised me when he laughed out loud. "I'll say."

"You noticed as well, then?"

"Everyone has noticed, sweetheart."

"What do you think it is?" I asked when we walked past the end of the bar and toward the office.

"I think he realized how much you mean to him. I'm sure he felt it before, but when we're faced with losing someone we love, the depth of our feelings becomes more apparent."

"He said as much. And apologized for not being more forthcoming with his feelings. However, this might take some getting used to."

"For me too." He leaned down to kiss my cheek. "I'll go see if there's anything I can do out front."

After looking through the two days' receipts, I joined him.

"You should take a night off," I said to Rebel.

"Oh, I will. Edge will soon insist on it. For now, though, I'm enjoying being here so much. The bar has gone from a place of really bad memories to a scene for making new good ones."

I felt the same way, but I didn't realize it until she voiced the sentiment. Rather than waiting for Cormac to walk in the door so I could exact my revenge, I was enjoying myself. There was a reason I fell in love with this place. In a way, it reminded me of Mary's, but there were many ways it didn't.

"Time for a dance?" Hammer asked.

"Absolutely."

He pointed to Kellen. "With him."

"Aye. You're right."

My brother seemed as surprised as Hammer had been the first time I asked him to join me. I reiterated the same story. "If you didn't dance at least once a night at Mary Donoghue's, you didn't belong there."

"Good philosophy."

"This is supposed to be fun, Kellen," I said a minute later when he didn't look like he was enjoying himself.

"I was wrong, Maeve."

"About?"

"This place. You. And selfishly, Texas is a lot closer to DC than Ireland is, so I should be glad you found this bar."

"It's the same for me. There were many reasons I came to America, as you know, but what you probably don't realize is that, in part, I wanted to be closer to you."

"Your turn," I said to Hammer after my brother and I had danced to several songs in a row.

"I didn't want to interrupt by cutting in."

As Hammer spun me around the dance floor, it occurred to me that I'd never been happier or more at peace in my life. I had him to thank for that; I just didn't know how.

<h1 style="text-align:center">31</h1>

Hammer

While the DA wasn't too happy about it, Fury appealed to Ringer, who relented and amended the amount of community service Maeve had to perform. Instead of one hundred hours for each charge, he changed it to one hundred total.

As she appeared to do with everything, Maeve tackled those hours with gusto. In less than a month, she was finished.

"Now what?" I asked when we left the courthouse, where I'd been a spectator rather than a participant in her final appearance.

"I'm thinking a visit to Billy and Alicia's is in order." Maeve turned to Fury. "Join us?"

"I would love to, except I have some Invincibles business to take care of. I'm also house hunting."

"To buy?" Maeve asked.

"Yes, but it has to require very little maintenance since my boss is dumping his entire workload on my shoulders."

"I've heard he's mean," I teased.

"Come on, meet us there. It's just lunch, and it'll be quick."

Fury gave in, saying she *did* have to eat.

"I wanted to run something by you," Maeve said once we were in the Porsche.

"Shoot." I winked and she smiled.

"I'm thinking that since we're moving forward with buying the bar, I might give up my place in Austin."

"Yeah? Where are you going to live?"

Maeve swatted me. "I'm moving in with you, Hammer."

"Is that right?"

"If you'll have me."

"How do you intend to earn your keep?"

She raised a brow. "I'd have to think about it. Do you have any ideas?"

"I do. After lunch, how about if we pick out a piano?"

"I see. Interior decorating, eh?"

"You know I'm hopeless at it."

"Sounds lovely."

Maeve ran her idea past Fury over lunch, and she begged us to take her to see it once we were finished eating. An hour later, the two women had reached a deal on a purchase price.

"I'll just need to move my clothes out," Maeve told her. "Most everything else came with the house, if you don't mind me leaving it."

"You'll get no argument from me. In fact, I think we wear the same size, if you want to leave your clothes too," Fury joked.

"I'll just pack a few more things now, then I'll come back later in the week to get the rest."

"Big move," I said once Fury and I were alone. "You sure you're ready to live in the city?"

"No offense, Hammer, but I don't think I could spend another month at your place."

"Have you actually been staying there? I thought you would've been at Rip's."

"That's cooled off quite a bit. We're both so busy."

According to Pete, who'd taken over for him, Rip had been gone the majority of the time since the hotwash. I also knew how busy Fury was, given the Invincibles' assignments still came through me.

"Let me know when it gets to be too much."

"And what? You'll take back over? Hell no. Plus, you've got your hands full with your new venture."

"About that, I have a contract I'd like you to look over for me."

"On or off the clock?" she asked with a wink.

"On," said Maeve, coming out of the bedroom. "Definitely, because it's my contract too."

Mac had kept us abreast of how Bobby was doing, who we'd learned was suffering from lung cancer. The last report Mac shared was positive, though. His brother had gone into remission, something the doctors said wasn't possible. When I asked if that meant he no longer wanted to sell, Mac said it was the opposite. Bobby didn't want to spend however much time he had left, working.

"He's anxious to get the deal done as soon as possible, so get movin' on that liquor license," he'd said the last time we talked.

I assured him that all I was waiting for was approval, which I believed would happen any day now.

"Send me that contract," Fury said, waving behind her as she walked to her car.

"Come on, Drip. We've a piano to buy."

"Can we get some other stuff while we're at it?" My house still looked like crap with the furniture I'd picked out.

"I thought you'd never ask."

32

Maeve

"The tune you're humming is so familiar to me," Kellen said during our flight to Dublin.

"I can't say. I don't even realize I'm doing it." However, Hammer's prior suggestion that it might be something I'd heard from my mum was making more sense.

I'd begun dreaming about her in ways I never had before. I had no idea if the dreams were based on memories or just what my imagination had conjured. They were lovely, though. In them, she often hummed like I did.

Last night's was particularly compelling, given in it, I told both her and my granny my intention to share the secret of the Tara Brooch with Kellen and Hammer.

Perhaps it was my subconscious assuaging my guilt, but in my dream, both women encouraged me to go ahead with my plan. The other thing that had happened in my dream was that when I apologized for leaving Mary Donoghue's, my mum reminded me she'd essentially done the same when she married my da and had me.

Granny even chimed in, saying that love should always outweigh a business.

"Love?" I asked.

"Of course love, Maeve. 'Tis easy enough for anyone to see you've met the man of your *dreams*."

I laughed now, remembering those words. My granny and my mum both possessed the same dry sense of humor as I did.

"What are you thinking about?" asked Hammer, who was sitting in the seat beside me.

I tightened the hold I had on his arm. "The Marys approve of you."

"Is that right?"

Kellen looked up from his computer and winked. "As do I."

"What about you, Maeve?" Hammer asked.

"It wouldn't matter to me if anyone approved or not." Both men laughed. "Let me finish."

"Go ahead," my brother said, still chuckling.

Like with so many things, I hesitated to say what was on my mind. It had always been easier for me to keep my feelings to myself, but I'd made a vow not to do that anymore.

"It doesn't matter whether anyone else approves or not, because I love him."

I looked into Hammer's eyes. Perhaps it wasn't a confession I should've made in Kellen's presence, but if I hadn't said it now, I might've talked myself out of saying it at all.

"You don't have to say it back."

"I don't?" He leaned forward and kissed me. "And what if I want to?"

"No one is stoppin' you."

Hammer cupped my cheek with his palm. "I love you, Mary Maeve Donoghue McTiernan. Very much."

"You do?"

"Very, very much."

Out of the corner of my eye, I saw my brother was no longer sitting across from us.

"This feels right." Before I could question what he meant, Hammer reached into his bag and pulled out a small black velvet box.

"I was wondering if you'd like to add another name after McTiernan. Will you marry me, Maeve?"

He opened the hinge, and inside was the most beautiful Claddagh ring I'd ever laid eyes on. It was made of black gold, and the heart clasped by two hands was a bright and vibrant emerald. In the crown above it were four diamonds. "It's so lovely," I said when he took it from the box. "Yes, I will marry you, *Sterling*. I think Maeve Anderson is the name best suited to me." He slid the ring on my finger, and it was a perfect fit. Just like he was for me.

"I think I remember where I heard that tune before," said Kellen in the car ride that took us from the airport to the original Mary Donoghue's in Dublin.

"You do?"

"Your mother used to sing a lullaby to you with the same melody."

My eyes opened wide. "She did?"

"I think it's being here in Ireland that brought the memory back to me." He was sitting in the front seat, while Hammer and I were in the back. He turned so he was facing me.

"I also remember it was the only thing that seemed to put you to sleep."

Hammer squeezed my hand. "Now you know."

I couldn't explain why I felt myself on the verge of tears. "I hope I'm doing the right thing," I said under my breath.

"Marrying me?"

"No. Of that, I'm certain."

"Glad to hear it."

"Hammer, have you been to Mary's?" I asked, realizing we hadn't talked about it.

"I haven't."

"I haven't either," said Kellen.

"Well, you are in for a real treat, then." I hadn't planned to go into the pub first, but as Hammer said earlier, it felt right.

To my delight, Michael Callahan was behind the bar. The man seemed as though he never aged, and he had to be at least eighty.

"If it isn't our own Mary Maeve!" he roared above the din of the crowd, coming out to greet me. "Welcome home, lass."

It seemed I knew everyone in the place as they came to greet Kellen, Hammer, and me.

"What is this?" asked Bridget, one of the barmaids, picking up my left hand. "Are you engaged, lass?"

"Aye." I put my arm in Hammer's. "And this handsome devil is my future husband."

The celebration of my homecoming flowed right along with the Black and Tans until last call. By then, it was too late to show Hammer and Kellen why I'd asked them to come to Ireland with me. Tomorrow would do. What I had to show them had remained where it was for generations. Another few hours would make no difference.

Kellen and I still jointly owned the house I'd grown up in, so that is where we stayed. Since the bed in my room was intended for one very small person, Hammer and I shared the room my parents used to sleep in. Even that bed was small compared to the one we slept in at the ranch, and I said so.

"You know, I've been thinking about the ranch," he said as we *cwtched*.

"Tell me you're not thinking of selling."

"No, naming it."

"Yeah?"

"The Hammered Dubliner."

I burst out laughing. "Oh, Lord, you are *tattered*."

"What?"

"You know, wankered, shit-faced, *drunk*."

"I'm not. I'm completely serious."

I laughed again. "We'll talk it over in the morning," I said before humming us both to sleep.

"Whatever is making you so anxious, we don't have to do, Maeve," Hammer said to me after I'd made a right mess of breakfast.

"I'd rather get it over with," I muttered.

Hammer got up from the table and stood behind me as I tried to salvage the fried eggs and tomatoes I'd burnt to a crisp.

"You're distracted."

"I've ruined breakfast."

Hammer took the spatula from my hand. "I can make more eggs, but with all the rest of this, I don't think we need them."

I'd wanted to make a traditional Irish breakfast, which consisted of rashers, bangers, baked beans, fried potatoes along with the aforementioned eggs and tomatoes. I'd skipped the black pudding because most outside of Ireland didn't care for it. It even turned my stomach.

"Maybe just eggs. No tomatoes."

He smiled. "Go sit down, and I'll handle it."

"I suppose I should've warned you I'm not a very good cook."

"That's okay. You're great at interior decorating." He wriggled his eyebrows. "Among other things."

"Something smells good," my brother said, joining us in the kitchen.

"Sod off."

"*What?* I'm serious."

"Your sense of smell is still drunk," I muttered, putting my head in my hand.

"You're probably right about that."

"Hair of the dog," said Hammer, pulling something from the icebox. "Callahan sent this with me."

He got out three pints and poured what I recognized as Irish Breakfast Ale.

"Feel better?" Hammer asked after I'd finished all of my breakfast, some of his and Kellen's, and downed two pints.

"Much. Come on. Let's get this over with." I motioned for them to follow me out of the house.

33

Hammer

"Where are we going?" Money asked when Maeve led us in the direction of Mary Donoghue's. Clearly, the pint he drank hadn't helped his hangover as much as it appeared to have helped Maeve's.

"Stop your whinin'. It isn't far," she told him. I laughed. He *was* whining.

"Maeve, I don't think I can drink any more alcohol this morning."

"It's a good thing that's not where I'm takin' you, then, isn't it?"

As she'd said, instead of going into Mary's, she led us across the street to a building that looked older than the pub, which would make it ancient.

Maeve pulled out a ring of skeleton keys from her jacket pocket, used one to unlock the door, and motioned for us to follow her inside. She lit a gas lantern and held it in front of her as she led us down a set of stone steps.

"What is this place?" Money asked.

"In a minute, you'll see," she muttered.

She unlocked yet another door that led to a second set of stone steps. When we got to the bottom, she asked me to hold the lantern. Instead of more keys, she took the Tara Brooch from her pocket and pulled the pin away from the penannular ring. I watched as she stuck it into a small hole in the wooden door. Like a key would have, the pin hit a mechanism, clicked, and it opened.

Maeve took the lantern from me and stepped inside.

"What is all this?" I asked as she shone the light on what looked like thousands of old coins.

Money picked one up. "*Gun money!* There must be millions of dollars' worth in here."

"Aye," said Maeve. "Millions and millions."

"What is gun money?" I asked, feeling like I should know, but didn't.

"James II issued it in the late sixteen hundreds in order to finance the Williamite War. Which he lost in the end."

"Not the first nor the last clash of Catholics versus Protestants in Ireland," added Maeve.

Money explained that James II, who was once the king of England, Ireland, and Scotland, used what became worthless currency to attempt to take back the kingdom from which he was overthrown by his daughter and her husband.

"Let me guess," I said, noticing the twinkle in Maeve's eye. "Her name was Mary."

She nodded. "Aye. That was her name."

"Donoghue?"

"Unofficially, yes. It was the name she and William used when they traveled."

"You said it became worthless?"

Money turned in a circle, taking in the largesse. "Then. It's been said there was no more left of the stuff."

"As you can see, that rumor is untrue."

"I don't know what to say," said the man I'd rarely seen speechless, although he wasn't prone to talking when it wasn't necessary either.

"I want it and the brooch to go to the National Museum," Maeve announced. "It's time they had the real one."

"You're sure?" Money asked. "It's part of your heritage."

"Aye, but what good is it doin' sittin' in here for hundreds more years?" Maeve turned to me. "What do you think?"

"What a wonderful gift this would be to your homeland."

She beamed. "I knew you'd understand."

Epilogue

Maeve
One Year Later

I'd insisted the donor of the brooch and the gun money remain anonymous. I suppose the director of the National Museum of Ireland believed I'd done it to avoid paying taxes or some such thing, but I hadn't. The way I saw it, none of it had ever truly belonged to my family. We'd just held onto it for safekeeping.

There was quite a scandal over the brooch, with scholars and scientists arguing over which one was authentic. It didn't matter to me, and since my identity was never revealed, no one questioned me about it.

I was sitting at the piano, attempting to piece together the music for the tune I so often hummed, when my husband walked in the front door.

"Did you see Rip?" I asked. The man had been away from the ranch for the better part of the year but had returned today, saying he needed a favor.

"I did."

"What did he want?"

Hammer rubbed his head with his hand.

"What? Just tell me, for *feck's* sake."

"Better have him explain. They'll be here shortly."

"They?"

"Yes."

I got up from the piano and joined him in the foyer when there was a knock at the door. Hammer opened it and invited Rip and a young woman inside.

"Maeve, it's so good to see you," he said, stepping forward to hug me. "Hammer didn't mention you were pregnant. Congratulations! When is the baby due?"

I rubbed my belly like my husband often rubbed his head, including a few minutes ago. "Next month."

"We're having a girl." Hammer beamed.

"Yeah? I'm so happy for you both."

"Please introduce us," I said, stepping forward to greet the woman who'd arrived with Rip.

"Maeve, Hammer, this is Pearl Fischer."

"It's nice to meet you," I said, stepping forward to shake Pearl's hand. "Fischer. Why does that name sound familiar?"

Both Rip's and Pearl's faces flushed.

I turned to look at Hammer. "What?"

"We'll talk later."

"It's okay. I'll tell her." The woman straightened her shoulders. "My father, John Fischer, was one of your kidnappers."

Keep reading for a sneak

peek at the next book in the

Invincibles series:

Ripped

1

Rip

The last thing I expected when Vex requested a meeting was that he wouldn't come alone. When I saw a woman in the passenger seat of his SUV, I was even more baffled.

"Who is that?" I asked when I got out of my truck and met him in between where we'd both parked on the bottom floor of the underground parking structure.

"A complication." He looked over his shoulder as if to make sure she hadn't gotten out of the vehicle. "Her name is Pearl Fischer."

"Any relation to—"

"Yeah, she says John Fischer was her father."

"Shit." The man was one of the two ABT members who'd abducted Maeve McTiernan—sister of Money McTiernan. Both men had been shot and killed during an "asset exchange," as it had been touted, that was really just a rescue mission. "Why is she with you?" And why the fuck was I here, I wanted to ask, but Vex would get to that—I hoped sooner rather than later.

I had a bad feeling about this and hoped my gut instinct was wrong.

"I was leaving an ABT meeting and found her hiding under my car."

"Wait. What?"

"You heard me. I might've run her over if she hadn't reached out and grabbed my ankle when I was getting in."

"Another way she could've gotten herself killed."

"Exactly. Anyway, when I knelt down, she begged me not to expose her. Said she was being kept against her will and needed to get off the compound."

"Risky."

"No shit. Turns out there's some unrest within the ABT."

"That's nothing new. I keep hoping one side will take out the other, so we don't have to."

"The way she saw it, her father was aligned with the new colonel in town—me."

The highest rank of any state chapter, such as the Aryan Brotherhood of Texas, was "major." At the bigger organization—the Aryan Nation—the highest rank was "general." Since Vex's cover was that he'd been the head of the Nazi Freedom Riders, who had merged with the national organization, he was given the second highest rank possible. He'd also been tasked with "cleaning up" the Texas chapter. However, with any prison gang made up of street thugs, the definition of cleaning up was up for interpretation.

I figured I might as well cut to the chase. "What am I supposed to do with her?"

"I need you to keep her safe until I figure out a better solution."

"Who does she think I am?"

"I know you from the Freedom Riders."

"Someone who didn't come over when you did?"

"Exactly."

"I'll repeat my earlier question. What am I supposed to do with her?"

"Contact Money and ask him."

Kellen "Money" McTiernan was the director of the Central Intelligence Agency. The organization I worked for, the Invincibles, was a private security and intelligence firm that McTiernan used for jobs that fell outside of what he could make happen within the agency.

"For now, take her with you to the safe house." Vex spoke as if he was in charge of this mission rather than the other way around.

"You said she was being held against her will. Why don't we just let her go?"

"Because she has no idea who she is."

"You just told me she's John Fischer's kid."

"Yeah, except there's no birth certificate on record for anyone named Pearl Fischer, nor is John Fischer listed on a birth certificate for any other kid."

I looked over at the woman waiting in Vex's vehicle. "Who is she, then?" I muttered more to myself than him.

"Good fucking question."

About the Author

USA Today and Amazon Top 15 Bestselling Author Heather Slade writes shamelessly sexy, edge-of-your seat romantic suspense.

She gave herself the gift of writing a book for her own birthday one year. Forty-plus books later (and counting), she's having the time of her life.

The women Slade writes are self-confident, strong, with wills of their own, and hearts as big as the Colorado sky. The men are sublimely sexy, seductive alphas who rise to the challenge of capturing the sweet soul of a woman whose heart they'll hold in the palm of their hand forever. Add in a couple of neck-snapping twists and turns, a page-turning mystery, and a swoon-worthy HEA, and you'll be holding one of her books in your hands.

She loves to hear from my readers. You can contact her at heather@heatherslade.com

To keep up with her latest news and releases, please visit her website at www.heatherslade.com to sign up for her newsletter.

MORE FROM AUTHOR HEATHER SLADE

BUTLER RANCH
Kade's Worth
Brodie's Promise
Maddox's Truce
Naughton's Secret
Mercer's Vow
Kade's Return
Butler Ranch Christmas

WICKED WINEMAKERS
FIRST LABEL
Brix's Bid
Ridge's Release
Press' Passion
Zin's Sins
Tryst's Temptation

WICKED WINEMAKERS
SECOND LABEL
Beau's Beloved
Coming Soon:
Cru's Crush
Bones' Bliss
Snapper's Seduction
Kick's Kiss

ROARING FORK RANCH
Coming Soon:
Roaring Fork Wrangler
Roaring Fork Roughstock
Roaring Fork Rockstar
Roaring Fork Rooker
Roaring Fork Bridger

THE ROYAL AGENTS
OF MI6
Make Me Shiver
Drive Me Wilder
Feel My Pinch
Chase My Shadow
Find My Angel

K19 SECURITY
SOLUTIONS TEAM ONE
Razor's Edge
Gunner's Redemption
Mistletoe's Magic
Mantis' Desire
Dutch's Salvation

K19 SECURITY
SOLUTIONS TEAM TWO
Striker's Choice
Monk's Fire
Halo's Oath
Tackle's Honor
Onyx's Awakening

K19 SHADOW OPERATIONS
TEAM ONE
Code Name: Ranger
Code Name: Diesel
Code Name: Wasp
Code Name: Cowboy
Code Name: Mayhem

K19 ALLIED INTELLIGENCE
TEAM ONE
Code Name: Ares
Code Name: Cayman
Code Name: Poseidon
Code Name: Zeppelin
Code Name: Magnet

K19 ALLIED INTELLIGENCE
TEAM TWO
Coming Soon:
Code Name: Puck
Code Name: Michelangelo
Code Name: Typhon
Code Name: Hornet
Code Name: Reaper

PROTECTORS
UNDERCOVER
Undercover Agent
Undercover Emissary
Coming Soon:
Undercover Savior
Undercover Infidel
Undercover Assassin

THE INVINCIBLES
TEAM ONE
Decked
Edged
Grinded
Riled
Smoked

THE INVINCIBLES
TEAM TWO
Bucked
Irished
Sainted
Hammered
Ripped

THE UNSTOPPABLES
TEAM ONE
Furied
Merried

COWBOYS OF
CRESTED BUTTE
A Cowboy Falls
A Cowboy's Dance
A Cowboy's Kiss
A Cowboy Stays
A Cowboy Wins